Praise for
Rachelle J. Christensen's
Award-winning Novels

Hawaiian Masquerade is the perfect summer read. Set on the beautiful island of Kauai, you will fall in love with the characters, the story line, the setting, and most of all the romance. I would highly recommend this fast-paced, fabulous clean romance.
—Cami Checketts, author of *The Feisty One: A Billionaire Bride Pact Romance*

Christensen has done a magnificent job of putting together an unlikely match and letting it challenge the characters to grow, change, and become better together than they were apart. This is a wonderful, sweet romance that you'll want to stay up to finish.
—Lucy McConnell, author of the *Billionaire Marriage Brokers* series

"Any reader who loves mysteries with a dose of romance, or romance with a dose of mystery, should not miss this book! The author seamlessly combines both elements into a sweet, exciting story, excellently written from start to finish."
—InD'Tale Magazine

"SILVER CASCADE SECRETS is an exciting romantic suspense novella … Great writing, a sweet romance, and an intriguing mystery all rolled into a single story."

THE
BILLIONAIRE'S
Stray HEART

BURKE BILLIONAIRE ROMANCE

Other Works by Rachelle

Diamond Rings Are Deadly Things (Wedding Planner Mysteries #1)

Veils and Vengeance (#2)

Proposals and Poison (#3)

The Soldier's Bride (A Music Box Romance #1)

Carve Me a Melody (A Music Box Romance #2)

Hawaiian Masquerade (Burke Billionaire Romance #1)

The Billionaire's Stray Heart (Burke Billionaire Romance #2)

How to Fetch a Fiancé (Destination Billionaire Romance)

River Whispers

Wrong Number

Caller ID

Novellas:

Silver Cascade Secrets

Double Take

Hope for Christmas: An Echo Ridge Romance

The Kiss Thief: An Echo Ridge Romance

The Princess Bride of Riodan: An Echo Ridge Romance

Coming Home to Love: An Echo Ridge Romance

Nonfiction:

What Every 6th Grader Needs to Know: 10
Secrets to Connect Moms & Daughters

Lost Children: Coping with Miscarriage

Ultimate Life: Create a Life Worth Living in 9 Simple Steps

THE BILLIONAIRE'S Stray HEART

BURKE BILLIONAIRE ROMANCE

Rachelle J. Christensen

FREE DOWNLOAD

Get Rachelle's novella, *SILVER CASCADE SECRETS*, for FREE.

"Great writing, a sweet romance, and an intriguing mystery all rolled into a single story."

—Heather B. Moore
USA Today Bestselling Author

Take one park in autumn, mix in a handsome stranger, a daring heroine, murder, chocolate peanut butter brownies, mystery, and a few kisses and you'll see why *Silver Cascade Secrets* has everything you need to satisfy your cravings for a good read.

Available on Amazon, Nook, Kobo, iBooks, and more.

Get your free copy when you sign up for
the author's VIP mailing list.

Get started here:
http://www.rachellechristensen.com

Dedication:

To the real Roxey, the shelter dog who inspired this story. I brought you home as a puppy and loved you through all the chewed up shoes and toys. Thank you for helping me make room in my heart for one more.

And thank you to my family, for having patience with Roxey and loving her wild and crazy behavior almost as much as me!

Chapter 1

Jordan Burke checked his watch as he walked from his office in downtown Chicago to the lunch meeting that would start in ten minutes. The billionaire owner of Burke Enterprises could have taken the company limo, but walking was faster in the midday traffic and it was a good excuse for him to get some exercise. He quickened his pace only to be held up by a red hand signal at the stop light. He tapped his foot impatiently as he waited for the light to change.

"Jordy! Jordy, wait up!"

Jordan straightened and then turned at the sound of the nickname that his sister, Lexi, still called him. A woman with dark hair pulled back in a ponytail tugged on the leash of two dogs that were fast approaching him. The border collie stayed alert at her side, but the larger golden doodle tugged on the leash, following his nose toward Jordan.

"Jordy. Heel." The dog hesitated, glanced at the woman, and then nosed against Jordan's hand.

"I'm sorry. This one's in training." She tugged on the leash again.

Jordan laughed. "His name is Jordy?"

The woman tilted her head and gave a hesitant smile. "Yes."

Jordan pointed at himself. "That's my nickname, but only my sister calls me that."

She laughed and Jordan noticed the musical sound—bright and beautiful, just like the light in her hazel eyes. "Well, don't feel bad. I've met lots of dogs named Maddie, which is my nickname. My friend told me I should take it as a compliment that my name is so popular for dogs."

Jordan laughed again and felt some of the tightness in his shoulders ease up. He patted Jordy's head, noting that his namesake had a curly golden coat that was well-groomed.

"This dog sure is a beauty."

She nodded. "He is that. His owners were considering giving him up because he was so hyper." She smiled down at the dog. "But you're doing better now, aren't you, Jordy?" She looked up at Jordan and her cheeks pinked. "I'm a dog trainer, so both of these guys are my clients."

Jordan's heart did something funny when he noticed her cheeks flush. It almost felt like it'd skipped a beat. He took a step closer to Maddie. She had a dimple in her left cheek and a small nose with a light smattering of freckles. "You must be good at your job then. Lucky guy." He rubbed behind the dog's ears, forcing himself to look away from the sparkle in Maddie's eyes.

"Thank you." The border collie shifted his weight back and forth and looked up at Maddie.

The street signal began chirping, and Jordan looked up to see the walk signal. "Well, good luck with those two." He lifted his hand in a wave and hurried across the street. Once his feet hit the sidewalk again, he hesitated, looking back once. Maddie had turned toward the park and for a moment Jordan wished he'd asked her for her phone number. He shrugged. Who was he kidding? He didn't have time to date. He glanced at his watch again and frowned. The old Jordy might not have worried about being late to a lunch meeting if it meant getting the number of a pretty girl, but that guy had been replaced by the new and improved version. Jordan Burke was a man of business.

Chapter 2

*S*even months. That's how long it had been since Jordan Burke's last date. His younger sister, Lexi, had done her best to remind him of that fact and persuade him to go on a date tonight. Jordan stood in the waiting area of the fancy Thai restaurant waiting for his date to show up.

His date was Lexi's best friend, Gracie Cardulo. Jordan hadn't seen her for at least three years, but he still remembered how beautiful she was with her lithe dancer's body, olive skin, and dark hair. He wondered if Lexi had twisted her friend's arm to schedule this date as well.

Jordan didn't really look at it as an actual date, but the thought made him wonder, if he had time to date, who would he go out with? His heart did that funny skip-beat thing again when the woman walking those dogs came to his mind.

Maddie. It had only been a few hours ago and he mentally kicked himself again for not getting her number.

"Well, you're actually here." Gracie sidled up next to Jordan, her face lifting in a familiar smile. Jordan snapped back to attention and smiled as he looked down at Gracie. "I'm here. But don't look so surprised. How are you?" He gave her a hug. They had texted back and forth in preparation for the date so Jordan knew that she'd traveled to Chicago to audition for a part in a ballet studio.

Gracie smiled. "Well, the auditions are over but I won't know for a couple more days whether I got the part or not."

Jordan's phone buzzed in his pocket and he reached to grab it, but paused when he realized that Gracie was waiting for him to reply. He cleared his throat. "Oh, well, I'm sure you'll get the part and if you don't, it's their loss."

Gracie put her hand on his arm. "Thanks for that. I really don't know what's going to happen with my career. I'm probably too old to try out for the part that I did."

Jordan raised his eyebrows. "Aren't you the same age as Lexi? Thirty-two, thirty-three? If you're old, what does that make me?"

Gracie laughed. "I'm only twenty-eight, but when it comes to ballet, old was a few years back. I'm really pushing it now. But don't worry, you have a lot of good years left in you." She winked.

Jordan's phone buzzed again and his lips twitched. "Do you mind if I get this real quick?"

Gracie lifted one shoulder and let it drop. "Go ahead."

Jordan looked at his screen and saw that the call wasn't coming in from China so he could ignore it for now. He swiped down sending an automatic text message and slipped the phone back into his pocket. "Sorry about that."

Before Gracie could answer, the maître d' arrived and led them through the dining area to a cozy table for two infused with ambient light. They had a few minutes to talk over the menu and place their order before Jordan's cell phone pinged with incoming texts. He shook his head, holding up the phone. "Work never stops." He hurriedly answered the texts and then slid the phone into his pocket. "So how do you like Chicago?"

"It's a beautiful city—so much history," Gracie answered. "I love that the arts play such a role here. Please tell me that you've taken time to appreciate some of that."

"I always meant to double with Lexi and her dates to some of the concerts and such, but then, she never dated much when she was here either." Jordan struggled to think of the last thing he'd done for fun that was unique to the city. "I can see the St. Patrick's Day parade from my office window."

Gracie leaned forward. "But I have a feeling you didn't see much of it this year."

"They dye the river green." Jordan tried to remember if he had even looked out his window this past March. He shrugged. "I guess I need to get out more."

"You said it, not me," Gracie replied. The answer indicated that his sister had filled her in on the sad state of Jordan's social life.

A few minutes later, their meals arrived and Jordan made an effort to ask Gracie specific questions that would take the focus off him. She explained the role she'd auditioned for in the well-known Swan Lake ballet. Jordan was about to ask her what her favorite part was when his phone started ringing again. He gave Gracie an apologetic look before pulling it out of his jacket pocket. "I have to take this—it's China. If you'll excuse me for a moment." Without waiting for Gracie to answer, Jordan stood and walked toward the back of the restaurant. He answered the call—another urgent matter concerning the new manufacturing plant in China that created molds for plastics.

When he ended the call he was surprised to see that it had taken him eight minutes to sort out the problem. He approached the table, trying to assess Gracie's mood before he sat down. She was toying with her salad, her brow furrowed as she gazed at the other diners.

"I'm really sorry about that."

"Don't you have a secretary or an assistant for phone calls?" Gracie asked.

Jordan nodded. "I do, but these are calls that have been transferred to me. Lately I'm fielding a lot more calls than I used to."

Gracie leaned forward. "That sounds like your assistant isn't doing their job. You need to hire more people, Jordan. You should be able to go out to dinner without fielding calls from China."

Jordan looked down at the fish on his plate, now growing cold. What she'd said was true, but he'd also started his company from scratch, running everything himself, staying up late every night trying to coordinate things with the difference in time zones from Chicago to China. "I probably do need to hire more help. It's pretty tricky finding someone with the right skill set, and especially someone who can speak Mandarin Chinese."

Gracie pursed her lips. "If you really wanted to, you could hire enough people that you would never have to answer another phone call from China. Or do you like having your phone be the boss of you?"

Jordan bristled. Gracie's words hit the target that others had painted on his chest—that he was a control freak, a micro-manager. He took a breath and blew it out. "Let's not talk about my job, that's boring." He straightened his tie. "So you said you're not certain what you're going to do next. If things don't pan out with this audition, where will you go?"

Gracie hesitated, as if trying to decide to let him change the subject. She set down her fork. "Lexi really wants me to come back to Kauai and work with her for Burke's Higher Steps. I'm just not sure I'm ready to retire from dancing yet."

Jordan opened his mouth to reply but was interrupted by the ringing of his phone. He groaned and looked at Gracie. She arched one eyebrow, cocking her head, almost daring him to answer it. He looked at the screen and recognized his main liaison to China. "I have to answer this. This is my second in command over in China. He never calls unless it's an emergency. He shoveled in a large bite of fish and mumbled. "Could you order us some dessert?" He hesitated with his finger over the screen waiting for Gracie to reply.

She sighed. "Go ahead. I'll order dessert."

Ten minutes later, Jordan gulped for air. He'd spoken as quickly as he could, people staring at him, possibly wondering how a blond haired guy in Illinois could speak Chinese. He sat at the table and his phone chimed with several incoming texts. He quickly scrolled through them, forwarding some for his assistant and answering others. He heard the clink of silverware and saw that Gracie had pushed aside her plate.

"Is dessert coming?"

Gracie licked her lips. She wasn't smiling. "I didn't order dessert. I think I'm just going to go. I can tell it's a really busy night for you."

Jordan panicked. If Lexi heard how he had treated her best friend...he groaned inwardly. He was in trouble no matter what he did now. "No, wait. I'm sorry. I'm just—I don't know what to do."

Gracie gave him a sympathetic look. "You know the saddest thing?"

Jordan straightened. "No. What?"

"You're a billionaire and yet you're working probably as many hours as you did when you started this business with nothing."

Her words poured down on him like acid rain. "Look, I'm sorry. I told Lexi I'm not in a place where I can date right now. You're a beautiful woman and I'm sure you're fun to be around, but I just don't have time to date right now. I hope we can still be friends."

Gracie stood and straightened her dress. "Friends? I don't think you're ready for friends either. Maybe you should start with a dog." She adjusted the strap on her purse and gave him a flat smile. "Thanks for dinner. I hope you have a good night."

Gracie took a step forward and Jordan's phone rang again. She glanced back as if giving him one last chance, but Jordan could recognize by the distinct ring tone that this call was more important than any other he'd answered that night. He lifted his fingers in a wave and put the phone to his ear answering in Chinese as Gracie walked out of the restaurant.

By the time Jordan paid the bill, ate another bite of curry and exited the restaurant, he had answered three more calls. He was angry with himself and also with Gracie's impatience. She hadn't seemed to understand that he really was the owner of a billion-dollar company.

Jordan was deep in thought as he walked down the street to where he had parked his car. He cut through an alleyway and walked about ten steps before he realized he'd made a wrong turn. He pivoted but his heart slammed into his chest when four young men stepped out in front of him.

"Okay, pretty boy, you know the drill. Hand over your cash." The hooded figure to his right spoke in clear English so Jordan couldn't pretend that he didn't understand.

Jordan hesitated, they weren't that far from the street entrance, but he didn't want to take his eyes off of the four gang members in front of him in case one of them made a sudden move. He swallowed, trying to come up with a response to keep things cool, but adrenaline pumped through his veins when he saw the glint of steel as one of them flicked a knife back and forth. He could easily throw his wallet out for them, but something told him that when they saw the 700 dollars in bills inside that he wouldn't leave this mugging unscathed. A guy who carried cash like that could be coerced for much, much more.

The alleyway was too dark. He couldn't tell if they had guns or not. Briefly he wondered if it was worth the risk to run to the other end of the alley. And then he thought of an idea. He began speaking rapidly in Chinese, putting his hand up and gesturing back and forth. When he paused to catch his breath, one of the young men took a step forward and held up the knife.

"Mister, we know you speak English. We heard you talking on the phone. Hand over your wallet and we'll let you go." The young man took a step forward and Jordan took a step back. He stepped on something soft, yet firm, and he heard a yelp, followed by a loud bark. Jordan stumbled into a pile of boxes, sending them toppling to the ground. They crashed across the alleyway and a vicious barking started up, different than the yelping at his feet. Jordan backed against the wall with the gang members shouting, demanding his wallet. His pulse drummed so hard he could hear it accompanying the sounds around him. The barking intensified as two large dogs streaked past him, ramming right into the gang members. Two of them fell to the ground and Jordan took advantage of the distraction, sprinting toward the end of the alley. With his breaths coming fast, he gasped when he saw the brick wall in front of him. A dead end.

Chapter 3

He turned around, fully expecting to see the gang members on his heels, but they were gone. The barking that had echoed along the alleyway was gone—the stray dogs must have kept up the chase. With a shuddering breath, Jordan retraced his steps carefully toward the street. There was no sign of the gang members. The young men must have fled when the dogs attacked. He wondered if the dogs had been asleep at the back of the alley and awoken when all the commotion started. Jordan looked carefully from side to side and was about to exit onto the street when he heard a whimper. It sounded like the yelping he'd heard when he stepped on something and stumbled into the boxes.

He turned to his left, crouching halfway and peered into the dim light next to the large dumpster. He could just make out the shape of a dog. Jordan took a step back, but the dog whined and let out a high pitched yelp. It inched forward until its black head was in the swath of the street lamp.

"Are you the dog I tripped on?"

The dog whimpered and wagged its tail, beating the side of the dumpster in a scattered rhythm.

"Are you hurt?" Jordan leaned forward, careful to maintain a safe distance between him and the dog. As his eyes adjusted to the light, he saw that the dog was actually just a puppy. A black lab puppy, by the looks of it. "Where did you come from?"

Jordan thought back to the two dogs that had ran past him, almost as if they were chasing something, or one chasing the other. Had they been after this puppy, hidden away in the boxes? When he'd stepped on the puppy, those dogs might have heard the yelp and gone after it. He realized with a start that this little puppy may have just saved his life. The puppy crept forward on its belly, as if trying to decide if Jordan was friend or foe.

"Hey, I'm not gonna hurt you. Come here," Jordan spoke softly.

The puppy lifted its head and when those dark brown eyes met Jordan's, his heart swelled with an emotion he'd hidden far away. He loved dogs, but no one knew that outside of Lexi. When his parents had died in a car accident almost five years ago, everything had changed for Jordan. But now, this puppy was staring him in the face, almost begging for help. "Let's get out of this alley."

Jordan put out his hand and let the puppy sniff it. The dog rolled over and Jordan noticed that it was a female. He tentatively scratched her belly and the puppy rolled back over with a satisfied yip. Once he was certain that she'd be okay with it, he picked her up. He carried the puppy to his car and used his phone to find an emergency animal rescue. When he explained that he would pay for all of her care and to have her spayed plus a sizable donation to the shelter, they said they could take her that night.

The puppy perked up on the ride through the city. Her pink tongue hung from the side of her mouth and it almost seemed like she was smiling at Jordan. There was a feeling in his heart—a twinge of something, but Jordan couldn't afford to listen to it.

He thought of what Gracie had said before she'd walked out of the restaurant—that he wasn't even ready for friends. That maybe he should start with a dog. Jordan smiled. He patted the puppy's head and she licked his hand.

"If I were in a different life, I'd take you home girl, but we'll make sure you're taken care of."

He was lying to himself and the dog because he was merely taking the easiest route to ease his conscience by getting the pup off the streets.

He pulled up to the animal shelter and lifted the puppy into his arms. She reached up and licked his cheek. Jordan laughed, remembering the times from his childhood when his dog, Ralph, had greeted him in the same way. He knocked on the door and an older woman answered. Her black hair was speckled with gray and pulled back in a tight bun. She wore a stained apron and a small golden cross around her neck.

"Well, good night if that isn't the most darling puppy. You say you found her on the streets?"

Jordan nodded. "She seems really friendly. I'm glad that you can take her. I wasn't sure what to do when I found her."

"Well, that's what we do here." The woman stepped aside to let him in. "Come on in. My name's Sue."

The door swung open and Jordan's nose twitched, the lingering antiseptic laced with dog brought back memories he'd long since buried. Ralph had come from a shelter like this one, and the memory made his mouth tighten. Jordan had stood beside his father, covering his nose, but the weird mixture of smells still filtered through. Dog hair hung in matted bunches to the mat by the door but when Mr. Farley brought Ralph out all Jordan could see was his dog. Ralph's entire body wagged with his tail and he yipped out a greeting that seemed to say, *I've been waiting for you to take me home.*

He backed up a step, but stopped when Sue tilted her head.

"Are you okay?" she asked.

He sniffed. "Sure. So um—I wanted to ask about a dog."

"Do you have a dog?"

Jordan cringed. "I used to. I'm not really in a position to have one now." He looked at the puppy and then carefully handed her over to Sue.

Sue shook her head. "Rules of the apartment. I suppose they get the best of us. But if things ever change be sure to visit us first. Shelter dogs have the best hearts. They can really change a person."

Jordan's throat tightened. The words were on the tip of his tongue to ask her how he could take this puppy home with him. But he swallowed them back. "Thank you. I'll remember that if my situation changes."

As Jordan drove back to his home in Lake Forest he couldn't stop thinking about the puppy and Gracie's words. His home had beautifully manicured lawns, a three car garage and plenty of space for a dog run. He grimaced when he thought about how much trouble he would be in when his sister learned about his failed attempt at a date with her best friend. Gracie had said that he needed to change things in his life. That woman at the shelter had said that a dog could help change someone's life. And then there was Maddie, the dog trainer he'd met earlier. She'd definitely approve of him getting a puppy. Too bad he didn't get her number.

He blew out a breath and tightened his grip on the steering wheel. He'd messed up every opportunity today. But still, the puppy might be an option. Jordan thought about going back to the shelter, but he shook his head. It would have been the perfect idea if his life and work were different. Even as he shook off the idea, he recalled the sandpaper-feel of the puppy's tongue against his cheek. His phone rang before he could dwell on the thought any longer.

Chapter 4

$\mathcal{M}$adison Poplawski knelt down and rubbed between the little puppy's ears. The black lab was friendly and sweet. "You're lucky someone had the heart to bring you in here."

The pup wagged its tail and Madison smiled as she continued to rub the silky black hair on the puppy's head. Sue had been on call last night so she'd admitted the puppy into the shelter and Madison was first to examine her that morning. The pup was probably about five months old judging by the teeth coming in. She was a mixed breed with a little bit of white on her throat and her belly, but she had a lot of lab in her. Her feet were webbed indicating that she wouldn't mind taking a bath the way some breeds did. And her eyes were brown, but they weren't the eyes of a purebred lab.

"I wouldn't be surprised if she's part border collie," Madison told Sue when she came in to check on her.

"Mm, hm, she'll be a cute one," Sue replied, patting the puppy on the head. Her gray scrubs matched Madison's, but the cuffs were almost worn completely through. "The man who brought her in sure was a looker, but he didn't want nothin' to do with a puppy."

"That's fine by me. The donation he made will be enough to carry us over to next month." Madison ran her hands along the puppy's back. She was malnourished and most likely had worms so Madison gave her the treatments, cleaned her up, and measured out a hefty portion of food for her.

It was just after 2 o'clock in the afternoon when the door chimed, indicating a visitor. Madison walked out front and her stomach flipped when she saw the blond man with sea green eyes. The guy looked like he could be in the running for People's Sexiest Man Alive. His white, even teeth peeked out from full lips that turned up easily in a smile. It was the guy she'd run into yesterday on the street—what was his name?

"Jordy?"

His eyes widened. "Hey, it's you. Maddie, right?" He was dressed in a business suit and everything about him emanated confidence and success. "So you walk dogs and work at the animal shelter?"

He remembered me! Madison swallowed and remembered that she was at work. "Madison Poplawski. I work here part time." She reached out to shake his hand. "Can I help you?"

For a moment a look of unease crossed his face, and then he took her hand. "I'm Jordan Burke and I came because…well, I'd like to adopt a puppy."

Madison bit back her surprise. His shoes looked like they probably cost more than two months of her salary and the way he'd strode purposefully across the street in a hurry the day before indicated that he was a very busy man. "Okay, what kind of puppy?"

Jordan cleared his throat, hesitant and then blurted out, "I'd really like the black lab puppy. The one that came in last night."

"How did you know?" And then Madison realized. "Are you the one who found her?"

Jordan nodded. "I just couldn't stop thinking about her, and I want to give her a chance."

"Well, I examined her and she seems to be in good health, but quite malnourished."

"What do I need to do? I've never adopted a dog before."

Madison took a closer look at Jordan. He was a business executive, but he was young, maybe only early thirties. He tapped the side of his leg unconsciously and Madison wondered if he felt a bit out of his element in the shelter. "Have you had a dog before?"

Jordan grimaced. "Yes. We always had a dog growing up."

Madison heard what he didn't say. She heard it because she had heard it in so many faces before. The pain of loss, the bond between a dog and a little boy that could never be broken. Jordan's eyes looked kind, but Madison was wary of this obviously busy and very wealthy man. Was he doing this to prove something to someone? She closed her eyes and reminded herself that not everyone was like her father. Madison looked up at him.

"Well, let's start by having you fill out some paperwork and then you can go and have a look."

19

Madison's blue tennis shoes peeked out from underneath the long hem of her gray scrubs in stark contrast to his expensive dress shoes. The metal clipboard scraped across the counter when she handed it to Jordan, the sound magnifying the pounding already at work at the back of her skull. He leaned over the counter and began filling it out.

"That's crazy that we ran into each other yesterday and now I'm here getting a dog," Jordan murmured.

Madison's heart cartwheeled at the low timbre of his voice. "It's funny how people bump into each other." It felt like eighth grade all over again—the cutest boy talking to her, and Madison left speechless. She chanced a look at him as he filled out the form.

Jordan was close to six feet tall with broad shoulders and a physique accentuated by his pinstriped suit. He looked up, catching her staring. He smiled and then refocused his attention on the paper. The back of Madison's neck felt hot and she turned and busied herself with a pile of paperwork in the inbox on the desk. She was curious about this Jordan Burke. On the outside, he seemed like a high-powered business executive, but his hesitant smile hinted at something different. A couple minutes later, Jordan slid the clipboard across the counter.

"Okay, can I see her now?"

"I'll be right back." Madison took the clipboard with her and stepped into the hallway. As soon as the door closed she examined Jordan's information. He was the owner of Burke Enterprises, an importing and exporting company in Chicago. He was thirty-six years old, single, and lived in Lake Forest—a ritzy suburb of Chicago. Funny, but when Madison had first appraised him, she would have never guessed he was the owner of a business. Something about that boyish look on his face—the way his hair was tousled in front, gave him an air of innocence underlying the confident façade. Or maybe she just thought that because she knew his nickname. Madison scanned the papers to see if there was anything else interesting and then she put the clipboard on the shelf. She walked back to the kennels and retrieved the puppy who squirmed excitedly in Madison's arms.

"Looks like you're luckier than I first thought."

Madison returned to the waiting room and put the puppy on the ground. She immediately bounded over to Jordan and yipped playfully. Jordan's face broke into a smile. "Well hello again. Did you miss me?" He knelt down and rubbed the dog's head.

Madison wouldn't have been able to explain it to someone else, but when Jordan knelt down and talked to the dog, it was like he became someone else. Or maybe a part of him shone through that wasn't there before.

"Do you know what you'd like to name her?"

"I've been thinking about it. What about Roxie?" Jordan asked.

Madison smiled. "That's cute. I think it fits her."

Jordan put both of his hands on either side of the puppy's face. "What do you think, Roxie? Do you like that name?"

The puppy reached up and did her best to lick Jordan's hands and face. He chuckled and Madison wished that she had more guts because this man was growing more attractive by the minute. He was handsome, intelligent, and he'd remembered her, but at the same time, he wasn't really flirting with her. Madison checked, but she didn't see a ring on his finger so maybe she shouldn't kick karma to the curb yet. Two chance meetings had to mean something right?

Home visits weren't always required, especially when the person appeared as well-qualified as Jordan. But since Madison was in charge she decided it wouldn't hurt to play on the safe side and check out Mr. Jordan Burke's living arrangements.

"First we do an inspection of your home and you're allowed a period of foster care if you'd like."

"Foster care?" Jordan looked back at the puppy. "So how long until I can adopt her?"

"Anywhere from one to two weeks," Madison replied. She leaned against the counter. "If you can show that you have everything you need to take care of her then we can complete the adoption within one week."

"I have a nice house and everything she needs. I went to the store before I came here and picked up a bunch of stuff."

"That's great. Do you mind if we set up an appointment to check out your home?" Madison ignored the way her stomach flipped when Jordan grinned at the puppy and then looked at her.

"Not at all. That's a great idea."

"Okay then. I actually have time tomorrow around two. I could come and do a home inspection," Madison said.

Jordan pulled out his phone and scrolled through his calendar. "I can make two o'clock work. So I'll just meet you at my house?"

Madison handed him the copy of the foster care agreement. "Just sign here and tomorrow I'll bring Roxie out and introduce her to her new home."

"I'll see you tomorrow then. Thanks for your help." Jordan rubbed Roxie's ears again.

Madison gave Jordan a list of supplies and suggested items that he might not have thought of on his first visit to the pet store. "This way you'll be all prepared for her arrival and the check-off will be quick and painless." She winked and then mentally shook her head. *Why am I flirting?* She felt Jordan's eyes on her and didn't dare make eye contact.

She picked up the pen that he'd used to fill out the application and put it back in the container. She felt drawn to him, but she wasn't sure why. He was handsome, intelligent, and successful but there was a vulnerable side to him that she'd seen when he held Roxie in his arms. Madison Poplawski had an unwritten rule about dating men who were married to their job—no exceptions. She was thirty-one years old now and the wounds of her heart seemed like they might never heal. Did she dare let her thoughts wander to Jordan Burke?

Chapter 5

ordan couldn't stop thinking about the woman at the shelter, Maddie, or Madison as she'd introduced herself, he remembered. What were the odds that he would run into her again in a city as large as Chicago? He had to admit that the chances were cosmic, but he wasn't really superstitious. Jordan wished that he had time for the parts of life he seemed to be missing out on—like dating—but he'd have to change a lot of things to get to that point.

He decided to concentrate on solving the problems at hand. He took Gracie's advice and hired two new assistants. One of them was put to work immediately, gathering all the extra supplies he needed for his new puppy, Roxie. There were quite a few things on the list that Madison had given him that he still needed to take care of. The other new hire was working alongside his second in command to figure out how to free up time in Jordan's schedule so that he wasn't plagued with hours of phone calls every evening.

Lexi hadn't called yet which meant that she either hadn't heard from Gracie or she was too angry to talk to him. At one o'clock Jordan performed what he thought was a superhuman feat. He left the office, not just for a lunch break, but for the day.

He met his new assistant, Cindy, at the house and she showed him how she had set up everything Roxie needed. A brand new doggie bed, a bucket full of chew toys, a package of organic puppy chow, and the puppy training pads didn't make up even half of the items she'd purchased.

For the hundredth time, Jordan questioned his decision to adopt Roxie. The secrets that he'd kept for nearly a decade gnawed at his heart. But even as his heart beat painfully around silent memories, he remembered what Gracie had said just before she'd left the restaurant. He wasn't romantically interested in Gracie, but it hurt that she had said they couldn't even be friends. It reminded him of all the times that Lexi had asked him to come to Kauai for a visit, and Jordan had told her he couldn't.

He had put his life on hold to build his company because that's what he had to do, wasn't it? His phone beeped with incoming texts, and five minutes later Jordan was still texting rapidly when his doorbell rang. Checking his watch, Jordan took a breath. Madison was here, and even though he knew it was because she needed to approve his house, he couldn't ignore the skip-beat of his heart. Walking toward the door, he finished a text and remembered his disastrous date with Gracie.

He pursed his lips, instructed his team to take a twenty minute break and pocketed his phone.

When he opened the door, his breath caught when Madison looked up and smiled. Her dark hair came to her shoulders in loose waves and she looked great in jeans and a light blue t-shirt. He suddenly felt overdressed in his shirt and tie. Madison held the squirming puppy and Roxie gave a little yip when she saw Jordan.

"Come on in," Jordan said, trying to act normal even though he couldn't seem to take his eyes off Madison.

Her dark eyes lit up as she smiled. "Thanks for agreeing to this visit. Would you like to hold Roxie? She sure is excited to be here."

"Hand her over. I still can't believe I'm getting a dog." He took the pup who immediately reached up and licked his face. Jordan laughed and noticed that Madison laughed along with him. He led her through the entryway and into the living room.

"Your home is gorgeous," Madison said.

"Thank you," Jordan replied. "I have an area set up in the mud room for Roxie. My assistant has been helping me get it ready this morning." He noticed Madison admiring the large living room and she gasped when they walked through the kitchen.

"This kitchen is to die for!" She ran her hand along the granite countertops. "Beautiful."

"Thanks. I'm thinking about trying to spend more time here," he joked, but recognized the truth in his words. Sometimes he slept over at the office when work from overseas kept him up until early in the morning. He shook his head. When had his work taken over his life? It hadn't happened overnight. There had always just been one more thing he needed to do. One more meeting, one more product to develop, one more company to buy. He stepped into the enormous mudroom and laundry room off the garage and held out his hand.

"Here's Roxie's new room." He pointed to the gates that had been assembled in the doorways. "This will be a temporary safety pen for her until she is house-trained."

"Wow, this is huge. Are you sure you don't want to adopt a couple more dogs?" Madison winked and Jordan breathed a sigh of relief.

He had passed the test. Whatever Madison was looking for, she must have seen it if she was suggesting that he adopt more than one dog. Jordan set Roxie down and the puppy scampered around the room, sniffing, tail wagging happily. She sniffed the edge of the training pad and promptly relieved herself partway on the pad and partly on the tiled floor.

"Good girl, Roxie!" Madison cheered. She looked to Jordan. "Can you believe she just went on the training pad like that?"

Jordan eyed the yellow puddle on the tile that hadn't quite made it on the pad. "I think I have a lot to learn, but that's a good thing then, even though she kind of missed?"

Madison chuckled and patted Roxie's head, feeding her a treat from a baggie she'd dug out of her pocket. "That's a very good start. If you can reward her immediately every time she even gets close to doing something right, she'll start looking for ways to behave and get her treat."

Jordan made a mental note to have Cindy work with Roxie later today. He was more than a little worried about taking the puppy on, but he couldn't resist the feeling in his chest swelling with love for the dog that could potentially mean a lot of trouble. He bent down and patted Roxie's head. "Good girl. You're going to be the best dog ever."

He turned and smiled at Madison who was watching him with a soft expression in her eyes. "I think you two are going to get along just fine."

"Thanks, I—" Jordan's phone let out a series of chirps that made them both jump. He pulled it from his pocket and quickly answered the urgent text message that had just come in. "Sorry about this," he mumbled.

Madison stood and tucked a strand of dark hair behind her ear. "If you'll just sign one more form, then I can be on my way."

Jordan tucked his phone back in his pocket, proud of the way that he'd quickly delegated the task so that he could concentrate on his guest. Madison was beautiful and Jordan didn't want this to be goodbye, but he wasn't sure how to extend the visit. "Thank you for coming out here. I promise I'll do my best to give Roxie a good home."

Madison nodded. "Just don't underestimate the amount of time and attention a puppy needs. You really shouldn't ever leave her unattended. Do you have plans for when you'll be at the office?"

Jordan wasn't sure, but it seemed like there might have been a slight edge to Madison's voice. He needed to let her know how serious he was about this new step in his life. "Yes, my staff is competent and I've actually hired a new assistant to help with Roxie. She's in good hands."

"I'm glad to hear that," Madison replied. "I hope you'll be able to give her the attention she needs too. There's something special about the way Roxie is already connected to you."

Jordan felt it too and it almost scared him, but he wouldn't let anyone else see that fear. He picked up the puppy and held her close. "Thanks for giving me a chance."

Madison nodded. "You're going to do great. Give the shelter a call if you have any problems."

"Would you mind if I contacted you directly? I mean—uh, could I have your number?" Jordan stammered and cleared his throat, feeling like an idiot.

Madison hesitated and then pulled out her phone. "Sure, what's your number and I'll text you right now."

"Great." Jordan rattled off the number and grinned. What he really wanted to do was ask Madison on a date, but that would take a little more courage and planning. They walked to the front door and Jordan showed her out.

"Enjoy your new puppy," Madison said.

"I will," Jordan said. He watched her walk to her car, still wishing he had the nerve to ask her out. Instead, he turned and walked back into his house. He took Roxie to the mudroom and texted his assistant that he was ready for her help. There were urgent matters he needed to attend to. He might even need to head back into the office for the rest of the day.

There was something about Jordan Burke that intrigued Madison and it wasn't just his clean-cut good looks. He surprised her with his genuine smile and the loving way he interacted with

Roxie was something that couldn't be denied. Madison could tell a lot about a person from the way they acted around animals—especially dogs. Jordan looked like he'd stepped back in time to a ten-year-old boy and his brand new puppy.

But there was more than that, something she couldn't discern, a sorrow that seemed deeper than the loss of his childhood dog, which he'd hinted at. The shadows of mystery around Jordan made him even more irresistible.

When she returned to the animal shelter, Madison pulled Roxie's file and reexamined Jordan's information. After a quick search on the internet, Madison's heart sank. Jordan was extremely successful, and very rich. He was thirty-six and one of Chicago's newest billionaires. Madison tucked the paper back into the filing cabinet and pushed away from the desk, the wheels on the chair squeaking across the linoleum. She couldn't allow her heart to be hurt by another man who only cared about work. Even as a little voice whispered that she didn't know Jordan Burke, Madison pushed him farther from her mind.

She thought of Abigail and her throat tightened. Her younger sister had been gone for six years. She could almost feel Abby's dark black curls in silky ringlets as she stroked her hair and sang her a lullaby. Madison clenched her fist and stood, heading back to the dog kennels. The animals' needs were always more than she could finish in a shift and that was good. Being busy was good, with not so much time to think. Except to think about her dream to start her own service dog training business. She focused on that dream and let all other thoughts fall away. It was safer that way, and safety was the only thing that kept the pain at bay.

 # Chapter 6

Two days later, Jordan arrived home just after seven-thirty as the sun was setting. His assistant had tended to Roxie at five o'clock, and assured him that the pup was doing well before she left. He had hoped to be home by six, but his work seemed to multiply by the minute lately. He loosened his tie and walked in through the garage. Roxie wasn't in her pen. The gate hung open against the wall. Jordan hurried into the kitchen. The house was quiet, no dog in sight. Jordan looked around the room and groaned. The edge of his leather sofa was chewed to shreds, the stuffing hanging out. The end table was knocked over and the once finely sculpted wooden leg now had several bite marks in it. He kept his cool until he rounded the sofa and tripped over the remains of his Santoni Italian leather shoes.

"Roxie! Where are you?"

Roxie bounded out happily from his bedroom, her tail wagging and Jordan's stomach sank. Did he dare hope that his bedroom was intact?

Jordan picked up his shoe and shook it at Roxie. "Why did you chew up my shoe? Look at what you did!"

Roxie cowered and whined softly.

Jordan sighed. "And what about my couch?" He pointed at the sofa and Roxie ran toward it, her tail wagging as if to say, *Look at what I did!*

Jordan shook his head. "What was I thinking? I can't have a dog."

Of course this would happen on his maid's day off. Maybe it was a good thing that the animal shelter had suggested a trial period with their foster care program. Jordan dropped his laptop bag on the table and pulled a Mountain Dew from the fridge. He filled a glass with ice and poured the soda over it. He tossed Roxie a piece of ice. She sniffed it, licked it, and then crunched it up in one bite. Jordan laughed and patted Roxie's head, receiving several slobbery kisses in return. The little black puppy had put several things in motion in his life, but Jordan wondered if he was patient enough, maybe he would see a real change begin. But then his eyes flicked to the chewed up shoe and he set his mouth in a determined line.

Tomorrow he was scheduled to call Madison and finalize the adoption. He would just tell her he had changed his mind—that it wasn't going to work out. Thinking of Madison made his brain go fuzzy. She was beautiful, and the way she looked at him made him want to be a better man. It was like she saw something in him that even he couldn't see. What would Madison think when he returned Roxie to the shelter?

Jordan shook his head. He already knew the answer to that. She would think he was a wimp. But he wasn't a wimp. He was a successful businessman—a billionaire. Burke Enterprises employed over three-hundred people and all of those people's lives were impacted because of *his* business.

"How can I run a billion dollar business and not be able to deal with one puppy?" Jordan let Roxie climb onto his lap and he stroked her silky ears. "We have to do something, but it needs to be the right thing."

Holding the puppy, Jordan sucked in a breath and walked down the hall to his bedroom. Surprisingly, it was mostly intact. "Good girl," he whispered as he rubbed Roxie's neck. It looked like the dog had slept on his bed—the white comforter had several black hairs on it—but none of the furniture had been destroyed. At least he'd arrived home in time to save his bedroom.

Jordan spent the evening cleaning up the mess with Roxie licking his ankles and tripping him as he walked from room to room. He fielded several phone calls as he cleaned and reminded everyone to work through his new assistants. They were still in training, but Jordan hoped that within two weeks, things might start to change in his schedule. He wasn't sure how he felt about that, especially since he'd been working at the same grueling pace for the past five years. He was worried that he might not know how to adjust to the change of pace.

Most of the mess was under control by ten o'clock, and Jordan was exhausted. He took Roxie outside for a few minutes and let her run off some of her energy and do her business. When they came back inside he checked every corner of Roxie's pen and shut her in for the night. "Stay here," he commanded, before patting her on the head and walking down the hall. Roxie whined, and Jordan turned and smiled at her. "You need to sleep there until you're housetrained."

It was already comfortable talking to the new little puppy, but Jordan hadn't figured out how to ask Madison on a date. Things had exploded with the new business he'd taken on in China, but truthfully his business wasn't the only reason. He was scared. Jordan hadn't pursued a serious relationship because of the baggage he carried, but he didn't like to think about that. Even so, as he slid in between the covers, Jordan's mind wandered to the night that his family dog, Ralph, had died. The same night his parents had died. He clenched his jaw and pushed back the painful memories. He was doing the right thing by taking this first step and letting a dog into his life again.

It was still dark when Jordan was awakened by a wet tongue lapping at his face at four-thirty in the morning. He groaned. "How did you get over that gate again?"

Jordan picked up Roxie and stumbled out of bed. He flipped on lights and went to check on her food and water dish. Both were full, but when he turned around, he discovered what she'd been up to. A white film dusted the entire kitchen. The pantry door was open and Roxie had drug out a sack of flour and chewed a hole in it. But that wasn't all. A box of cheerios and a bag of pretzels dotted the hardwood floor and right in the middle of that décor was a steaming pile of dog poop.

"That's it!" Jordan cried. "I can't do this." The memories from last night taunted him, and he pushed a hand through his hair. Why did he think this would work? His life had changed forever the night his parents died and no amount of work, good deeds, or shelter dogs could right the wrong that had haunted him ever since.

He locked Roxie up, cleaned up the poop, but left the rest of the mess in the kitchen. He called for his driver to pick him up, took a shower, got ready for work and then put Roxie in the brand new dog kennel his assistant had purchased for him. Madison had mentioned that her shift started at six o'clock in the morning. She took care of all the dogs, monitoring them for illness and getting them ready for future adoptions. At five-fifty-five a.m. Jordan's driver pulled in front of the animal shelter.

"I've got this. Just wait here." Jordan instructed his driver as he hauled Roxie out of the car and knocked on the door. Madison opened it with a wary look. Her hair was pulled back in a ponytail. Her eyes widened when she took in Jordan and the dog carrier.

"Come on in."

As Jordan crossed the threshold, he realized that she hadn't asked him what he was doing there so early in the morning. Guilt settled in. How many people reacted the same way he did? Taking a dog home, thinking they knew what they were doing and then returned it a few days later.

Madison watched him cautiously. "I take it things haven't been going to well."

Jordan frowned, shaking his head. "I don't know what to do. She's destroyed my house. You should see it!"

A glimmer of a smile tickled the corners of Madison's mouth. "Let me guess, shoes? Furniture? The garbage can?"

Jordan lifted his head and a little of the tension eased off his shoulders. "Not the garbage can, but everything else." He stood and paced back and forth across the small room. "Look, I feel terrible but I just don't know how I can make this work. I spend a lot of hours away from home and she needs someone who can take care of her—day and night."

Madison crouched down and opened the door of the kennel. Roxie jumped out, her tongue lolling to the side. "What she needs most is someone who can love her." Madison rubbed Roxie's head while the little pup twirled around in circles.

"But if I can't take care of her, why does it matter if I love her?" Jordan paused and looked at Roxie.

As if Roxie could understand his frustration, she walked toward him and sat down on his shoe. Jordan smiled. It was true what Madison said. The little dog did need love—a lot of love since he'd found her abandoned on the streets of Chicago. But what he had said was also true.

"Jordan?" Madison stood uncertainly, squeezing her hands together in front of her.

Jordan was struck with her natural beauty. He wished he was here asking for her number instead of showing her what a loser he was. He sighed. "Yeah, you can tell me I'm not qualified. I already know that."

"No, that's not what I was going to say. I was going to say that I saw something in you the first day when you came to ask about Roxie. I know it might sound funny, but I think you two need each other."

Her words hit the wall around his heart with a thud that jolted him backwards. The evidence that Roxie couldn't stay was everywhere, and yet when he looked at the little pup, into her light brown eyes, the wall around his heart shuddered. "I'm sure there are tons of families who would love a little dog like

Roxie. She'd probably have a lot more fun in someone's yard instead of demolishing my house."

Madison motioned to Roxie. "I just don't want you to give up too soon, before you have a chance to find out why you need her."

Jordan let her words sink in, wondering if she really meant them or if it was just some rehearsed pep talk that she gave every potential pet owner who brought their animal back to the shelter. He studied her, the way a lock of her dark hair fell across her hazel eyes. She was either a really good actor, or her words had been sincere. But what did that mean for Jordan and Roxie? He looked down at Roxie and her brown eyes tugged at his heart.

"Well, even if I wanted this to work, I don't see how it possibly can."

"I have an idea," Madison said. "I could help you train her. She *is* still a puppy, but at six months old, she's smart enough to do a lot of things *if* you know how to train her."

"So, I could hire you to train her?" Jordan heard the hopeful note in his voice but he didn't care.

"You can hire me to train her, but you have to work with us. It won't do me any good to train her if you don't know how to work with her."

Jordan frowned. He'd already wrung his schedule as tight as he could, or at least it felt that way. And now Madison wanted him to add obedience training on top of everything else?

As if reading his thoughts, Madison took a step forward, putting her hand on his arm. "I know it sounds like a lot. It probably sounds impossible, but three times a day you'll work with her for ten minutes at a time, or less. With just a few one-hour sessions, I'll teach you what you need to do in those ten minutes."

Jordan looked at the soft curves of her cheeks and the sparkle in her dark eyes. He wanted to spend time with her. There must be some way he could create an opening in his schedule for this beautiful woman. His heart thrummed with the possibility. "But what about your job here?"

"Well, I probably log enough hours for a full-time job, but this is a part-time position." Madison smiled. "I do a lot of training for other clients."

"Why didn't you mention that in the first place?" Jordan asked.

"Because it's a separate business from the shelter and I have to be careful about how I approach new clients."

"Okay, I get that." Jordan patted Roxie's head, giving himself a moment to realize that Madison didn't think he was a lost cause. And that meant a lot to him, even though if asked he would deny it. He looked up and smiled at Madison. "When can we start?"

Madison laughed. "Let's take a look at my schedule. The sooner the better. And Jordan?"

"Yes?"

"Go ahead and lock Roxie up in her kennel at night. She won't mind sleeping in there and then she won't destroy your house in the middle of the night."

Jordan grinned. "I think I have a lot to learn."

 # Chapter 7

The next day Madison headed out to Jordan's house again for their first training session. He sounded kind of stressed when he told her that he could only train for thirty minutes and then he had to get back to his office. She'd offered to come later, but he said that three-fifteen in the afternoon was the only time that would work for the next five days. Madison figured that meant that he must have a girlfriend who he spent every evening with. Too bad, he was definitely easy on the eyes and her heart kept standing at attention every time she thought about him.

She drove up the lane to his house and parked in the oversized driveway next to a fancy black car that might have been a Mercedes. It probably belonged to Jordan which was a good sign. He'd sounded so busy that she wondered if he would be late. She'd been to some beautiful homes before, but

Jordan's was definitely the nicest. And home didn't really seem like the right word for the mansion that rose up above the trees surrounding it. Grabbing the zipped bag of tuna fish, Madison got out of the car and walked toward the front door.

The door swung open just as she lifted her fist to knock. "Come right in. Mr. Burke is ready for you." A middle-aged woman dressed in a maid's uniform greeted her.

A mansion and a maid. Yep, he really was a billionaire. Madison stepped inside the foyer and walked toward the living room where she'd seen Roxie the last time she was here.

"Over here, Madison," Jordan spoke from her left.

She started and turned the corner to a large den. "Hi."

Jordan wiggled his foot, where Roxie was busy trying to chew his shoelaces. "Thanks for making this work." He reached out and shook her hand.

His palm was warm and his long fingers engulfed her small hand. At his touch, Madison's breath caught in her throat. He was dressed for the office in a gray button-up shirt and matching slacks. He was so good-looking that Madison stared a moment too long at his face. She noticed how the strong lines of his cheekbones stood out above the bit of scruff that ran along his jawline. "I'm happy to help you with Roxie today."

"This is Aaron," Jordan pointed to a young man behind them that Madison hadn't noticed because she was too absorbed with Mr. Billionaire's soulful eyes. "He's my video tech and he's going to be videoing what you teach me today so the rest of the staff can work with Roxie."

"Wow, okay. That's a great idea, actually," Madison responded. The guy looked like he knew what he was doing. Several of her clients had mentioned that they wished they had a video of her working with the dogs. She shouldn't be surprised that Jordan had a videographer here for the session.

"I thought it might be a good idea for when I'm gone to China or if things are too busy for me to work with her in the day to day," Jordan said.

Madison lifted her chin and put a hand on her hip. "It's a great idea, but if you're intending to excuse yourself from any training with Roxie, it won't work."

"What do you mean?" Jordan looked genuinely confused. "Training is training no matter who does it."

"That may be true to a point, but dogs are smart and they learn exactly what they can get away with for each person they interact with. You have to work with Roxie on a regular basis if you want her to be a well-behaved dog."

Jordan opened his mouth and then closed it. He pressed his lips into a thin line and looked down at Roxie. The puppy looked up at him and Madison saw the moment their eyes connected there was a subtle softening in Jordan's posture. He intrigued her, even as she concentrated on playing the part of the dog trainer. The love he already felt for the puppy was adorable. Madison took a step closer to him, her heart urging her to find out more about this man.

He reached down and patted Roxie. "Okay, I'll do whatever it takes. How much training time do I need to block out?"

Was he really that busy? Madison studied him and fear flared in her chest. Jordan was married to his job, so why was her heart trying to betray her? She snapped back to business mode. "We need to meet at least one hour a week for the first month and you should work with Roxie at least ten minutes in the morning and the evening. Your staff can work with her at different intervals during the day—each for ten minutes at a time."

Jordan looked up at her and smiled. "Okay, boss. I'll do my best."

His clear green eyes pierced her business armor and set her heart to fluttering again. Madison couldn't resist matching his brilliant smile. "Let's get to work then."

Chapter 8

After the training session, Jordan worked in the back seat of his Mercedes while his driver navigated the traffic back into the city. Jordan planned to put in another eight hours of work before he ended the day. He kept thinking about Madison, the way she moved, how her mouth quirked upwards when she teased him about being too busy to play with his puppy. The instruction Madison gave him was simple and Roxie had responded immediately when she sniffed the bag of tuna fish.

Jordan smiled, and then frowned. He didn't want to mess this up, but he wasn't sure how to create time for more training sessions with Madison. As if his sister could read his thoughts all the way from Kauai, his phone beeped with a long string of text messages. He glanced through them, laughing at the angry emojis Lexi had littered her text with.

I'm really upset with you Jordy, but I'm not going to let this ruin my vacation with Derek. I'll call you next week and you'd better have something great planned to fix this.

Jordan groaned. It had only been a matter of time until Gracie filled his sister in on all the gory details of the date disaster. But wait, he sat up straighter, what if he told Lexi there was someone else? Another date, and a puppy to go along with it. His sister would probably fall off her chair. Jordan laughed until he remembered he hadn't found the nerve to ask Madison out yet. Better fix that fast.

Once he reached his office, he met with his personal assistant, Porter, and was briefed on the top fires that needed to be put out. Before the meeting wrapped up, Jordan remembered Lexi's text and leaned forward, intent on fixing the mess he'd caused any way he could.

"Porter, how are things looking with this quarter's donation to Burke's Higher Steps?"

Porter pulled out a sheet of paper from his folder and passed it over to Jordan. "We'll be matching Lexi's donation of 250,000 dollars and contributing to the fundraising efforts in Georgia."

"Good. I gave a donation to the local animal shelter the other day, but I'd like to do more. Can you look into the foundations here that work with the animal shelters?"

"I'm on it."

Jordan nodded as Porter left his office. He wasn't donating to Lexi's foundation just to stay in her good graces; he truly enjoyed giving. He wanted to do more to help his community. He loved Chicago and there were so many worthy causes. One of Porter's assignments was to investigate exactly how the funds were used so that Jordan could be certain his money was benefiting the cause it was supposed to.

Giving money was great, but there were dozens of foundations each year that asked for his time, and lately Jordan had turned down every request. He hated saying no, but he didn't know how to change things or create more time for himself. He scrolled down though the report Porter had sent over, trying not to hear Lexi's voice reminding him that he had all the time in the world but he had the authority to choose how to spend it, just like money. He flicked through his schedule again and looked for any openings. His calendar looked like it had been drenched by a rainbow with slots in every color indicating live meetings, conference calls, employee training, department meetings, video conferences, and travel to China. All of those colors swirled into ropes that coiled around him and bound him to work every waking minute. Jordan clenched his fist. How had it come to this?

It felt like it was too late to make a change, but Jordan couldn't ignore the evidence that his life wasn't his own. His father's words of caution about finishing college and learning how to run a business haunted him, and Jordan pushed away from his desk. Lexi had walked away from everything and she seemed happy. Jordan didn't want to walk away, but he wanted to go home before ten o'clock at night. Madison had suggested that if he wanted to see real improvement with Roxie he needed to work in a training session once a week, as well as time every day. For now, Jordan had assigned his house staff with the duty of babysitting Roxie. They had a list of commands they were supposed to practice with the puppy, but

Madison insisted that Jordan spend quality time with his new dog too.

A beep emanated from his computer—the five minute warning for his next meeting. Jordan sat in front of his computer and drafted an email to his assistants. He sent a directive to his new office advisor, Shawn Halstrom, and asked him to challenge everyone on his staff to find something in his schedule that he could offload to someone else. He upped the challenge by asking them to create an escape route for him so that he could leave the office by six. Finally, he told Porter that every Tuesday for the foreseeable future, he'd be leaving the office at four-thirty to work with Roxie and his dog trainer.

After he hit send, Jordan felt a new energy building inside him—one that he didn't recognize. It took him a moment to identify the shift in his breathing, the looseness in his chest. *Is this what freedom feels like?* he thought. If so, he wanted more of it.

# Chapter 9

The rest of the week flew by, but Jordan remained intent on making changes in his schedule. There were a lot of protests, but he'd found a way to block out three evenings a week and that felt like nothing short of a miracle. He'd texted back and forth with Madison and he felt more comfortable around her, but he still hadn't asked her out. Today was their second official training session, and Jordan wasn't sure who was more excited—him or Roxie.

He arrived about fifteen minutes early and hurried to change into jeans and a t-shirt. Madison wanted to work with Roxie in the yard today, so Jordan took the puppy out front just as Madison pulled into the driveway. Jordan's heartbeat double-timed when Madison stepped out of her car. She wore dark pink yoga pants and a green tank top. Her dark hair was pulled back into a ponytail and the ends of it tickled the back of her neck as she leaned forward to shut her door. She turned and caught him staring. Jordan lifted his hand in a wave.

"Hi, Roxie sure is excited to have a visitor."

Roxie barked and jumped around Madison's feet as she approached. Madison giggled. "We have a lot of work to do today. Shall we go around back?"

Jordan nodded. "Come on, Roxie. Right this way." He took Madison through the side gate of his expansive backyard.

"Wow, this is beautiful. I didn't know you had this much property." Madison looked around the yard and Jordan noticed when she paused to study the wishing well next to the lilac bush. "This is darling."

"My sister got that for me after our parents died."

Madison turned to him, her eyes widening. "I'm sorry. I didn't mean to pry."

"You weren't. It's okay. It's been almost five years." Jordan wasn't sure why he had brought up his parents, but something about Madison's presence made him feel human again instead of a business machine trapped behind a desk.

Madison touched his arm. "I'm sorry for your loss, no matter how long it's been."

"Thank you." Jordan was about to say more when Roxie jumped up and grabbed hold of the hem of his t-shirt.

"Hmm, that is a problem," Madison said as Jordan tugged on his shirt, covered in slobber and two holes from Roxie's teeth.

"First off, we have to do something about this jumping," Madison said. As if on cue Roxie jumped up, her nose coming to Madison's shoulder. Madison turned and grabbed hold of

Roxie's front paws in midair. She squeezed Roxie's paws and the puppy winced.

"Roxie down. Keep your feet down," Madison said each word with emphasis and then she started walking forward, forcing Roxie to dance around in a circle. The puppy winced again and Madison let go.

Jordan arched an eyebrow. "So you didn't tell me you can dance."

Madison laughed. "I suggest you learn this doggie dance too. She needs to know that you don't want her to jump up on you either. Would you like to try?"

Jordan shrugged. "Okay."

"Now, when she jumps up, grab her paws and squeeze them gently. You don't need to squeeze too hard, just a little bit of pressure is uncomfortable enough to help her remember."

Jordan walked about five paces away from the middle of the lawn. "Come on, Roxie."

The dog came running and as soon as she reached Jordan's feet she jumped up with as close to a grin as could be on a dog's face. Jordan reached out and grabbed her paws and mimicked the dance that Madison had showed him. Roxie's eyes were expressive, curious and perturbed about doing this dance again. "Roxie, down! Keep your feet down. Roxie, down." Jordan enunciated each word and then he let go of Roxie's paws.

"Now be ready. She'll probably try again here in about ten seconds and I want you to repeat the same thing and the same commands." As soon as Madison spoke, Roxie's ears perked up and she looked from Madison to Jordan.

"Now say something to engage her."

"Roxie, are you a good girl?" Jordan asked. Roxie's tongue hung out the side of her mouth. She circled Jordan and leapt straight up towards his face. He barely grabbed her paws, but was able to repeat the same silly dance and commands to Roxie.

"Good work." Madison grabbed Roxie's paws. "I want you to be religious about this dance. Don't let Roxie jump up without you reprimanding her and when she stays down be sure to reward her. Tell her good dog. Yes. And give her a doggie treat."

Madison crouched down and looked toward Roxie. "Come here, girl." Roxie bounded over and as soon as she got near Madison, she licked her face. Madison stood and ended up repeating the same dance routine with Roxie, rewarding her at the end with a doggie treat.

"I'm sure my visitors will appreciate this new skill," Jordan said.

"Yes, from what I can see, Roxie will be happy to jump on anybody who gets close. You're going to have to work really hard with her. I suggest you have a few visitors over that aren't afraid of dogs who can help you with this lesson. You need to work on this constantly. Every time she jumps, be ready. I also want to work on some leash training so you can take her for a walk. Labs have a ton of energy. And for the first five years of their life they're like an entire classroom of mischievous boys rolled into one."

Jordan chuckled. "Sounds like a challenge."

Madison put one hand on her hip. "It is. Are you up for it?"

The way she looked, standing there with her hand on her hip did something to Jordan's insides. "I'm up for it. As long as you're here to train me."

Madison smiled. "I'm here to train Roxie. I don't think I'm qualified to train you."

Jordan grinned. "My sister did tell me I was a lost cause a long time ago."

"Does she live around here?"

"No, Lexi lives in Hawaii. She moved there last year and she tells me every chance she gets how much I'm missing out."

"Well, if she moved from Chicago I bet that's quite a difference."

Jordan nodded. "Yes, she moved during the dead of winter. So the contrast was pretty spectacular, or so she says."

Madison closed her eyes. "That sounds heavenly. Especially after the brutal winter we had last year."

Jordan laughed. "Maybe someday I'll get there."

"Wait a minute." Madison held up her hand. "Are you saying that Mr. Billionaire hasn't been to Hawaii?"

"I've been to Hawaii, just not to Kauai." Jordan put his palm against hers and gently pushed it down. "Besides, it takes a lot of work to be Mr. Billionaire." He waggled his eyebrows and Madison laughed.

Jordan joined her in laughing and Roxie decided that was a good time to jump on both of them again. As they repeated the dance technique, Jordan turned to Madison. "How did you learn so much about training dogs?"

"It's just something that I've always been interested in. I took every class I could and I worked with our dogs a lot growing up." Madison chucked a chew toy out onto the lawn and Roxie chased after it.

"What kind of dog did you have?"

Madison hesitated. This was the point in the conversation where she could let Jordan in, or give the answer that didn't expose any of her heart.

"I'm sorry if that's painful for you," Jordan said. "I still miss my dog too."

Madison hadn't realized how long she'd hesitated in answering his question, but Jordan was too perceptive. He'd somehow picked up that his question had skirted the edge of a painful memory. She looked up at Jordan and smiled. "A cocker spaniel named Copper. She was a part of the family and I don't think she ever really left my heart."

Jordan smiled. "Spaniels are fun. Did you learn about training from working with that dog?"

"Yes, she was a companion for my younger sister. Abigail had severe epilepsy and Copper always knew when she was going to have an episode."

"So she was like a seizure dog?"

"Yes, but we didn't call her that. Copper hadn't been trained for that kind of work, but my mom says that God sent her to our family for Abigail."

"That's really neat. I've read about how dogs can sense things like that. There was an article that explained how the dog can even retrieve a bite block for the person and protect them from danger during the seizure—fascinating stuff."

Madison nodded, her chest warming with Jordan's enthusiasm and understanding of something that most people had never heard of. "Copper was connected to Abigail like nothing I've ever seen before."

"So does Abigail have a new dog now?" Jordan asked.

Madison looked at the ground. "Abigail died ten years ago. She was fifteen."

"I'm so sorry. That was rude of me to ask." Jordan put his hand on Madison's arm and she felt a current of warmth travel up her arm and into her heart.

"It's okay. How could you have known? Abigail's life was hard, but Copper helped so much. It's one of the reasons that I want to start my own service dog center." Madison almost clapped a hand over her mouth. She never told people about her dream and somehow she'd just blurted out the most sacred parts of her soul to this man that she barely knew.

"Wow, that sounds like a fantastic idea," Jordan responded. "Is that something you've been working on?"

"Yes, and no," Madison replied. "I've done a lot of research on what I'll need to get started but—well, there's still a long ways to go." Madison had almost said that her biggest hurdle was money, but then she remembered she was talking to a billionaire. Would he think she was bringing up money because she hoped for a donation? Jordan seemed so easygoing that Madison kept forgetting how successful he was. "I could probably learn a thing or two from you on business."

Jordan brightened. "Maybe, if the lesson was on how to work so hard that you have no life and your sister is afraid you'll end up alone like Ebenezer Scrooge."

Madison chuckled. "I don't think you need to worry about that."

Jordan reached down and scratched under Roxie's chin. "You might be surprised at how close I am to Lexi's prediction."

"Now I'm curious. Do tell."

Jordan stood and rolled his shoulders back. "I might as well tell you because you already know I can barely handle a puppy for one night."

His eyes twinkled, and Madison took a shaky breath. The space between her and Jordan grew smaller. She leaned forward. "It's almost been two weeks now."

"True." Jordan laughed. "The night I found Roxie, I tried to go out on a date with one of my sister's best friends and she walked out on me because I was fielding calls from work."

Madison gasped. "That's a bit harsh."

Jordan held up his hand. "No, if she had slapped me and dumped her glass of wine on me, that wouldn't have been harsh because I was totally preoccupied and pretty much made her eat dinner alone." He dropped his hand. "I was a total jerk."

Madison rubbed the back of her neck. She had seen the signs and tried to convince herself that Jordan wasn't like other men—not like her father. He was a billionaire, which meant he had to work a ton, but maybe there was a chance that Jordan didn't want to work his life away. She took a shaky breath and decided to push the issue. "So you really are a workaholic then? You always put your job first—even before people?"

Jordan hung his head. "That sounds terrible. It's not who I want to be." He lifted his gaze to hers. "I've made a lot of changes in the past two weeks and I'm following through on creating a different life. I have no idea why I'm telling you this, by the way."

"I guess I'm like your dog therapist and you need to unload some of your issues?" Madison teased.

"Or maybe you're just really easy to talk to," Jordan said. "Thanks for listening."

His eyes were a vivid green and Madison focused on him and the words he'd spoken. "Thank you for listening to me too. I don't usually tell people about my crazy dreams."

"I don't think they're crazy at all. You're very talented and you seem to love what you do."

"But loving something and starting a business are two different things."

"Yes, but you're already running a successful business." Jordan motioned to Roxie and tilted his head. "How many clients do you have?"

Madison shrugged. "It varies, but right now I have fifteen."

"Fifteen?" Jordan looked impressed. "And you meet with them every week?"

"A few of them I meet with twice a week." Madison could feel something in the air between them. Jordan was opening up to her in a way that she doubted he had to anyone before, and all she wanted to do was stay and talk with him, to be close to him.

Jordan whistled. "Sounds to me like you're already halfway there."

Roxie yipped and Jordan and Madison both crouched to pet her, their shoulders bumping. Jordan smiled at her and Madison grinned back, savoring the moment where she could talk to a handsome billionaire and not worry about getting hurt.

# Chapter 10

*J*ordan kept his finger hovering over Madison's name on his phone. He'd composed no less than ten texts and deleted them all. He put down his phone and then picked it up again. Before he could start composing another text, Lexi's face appeared on the screen. Jordan hesitated half a second before manning up and answering it.

"I'm sorry."

"Jordan Burke. I can't believe you. I mean, I know I tease you about being Scrooge, but that doesn't mean you have to act the part!" Lexi's voice was one part frustration mixed with two parts disappointment.

Jordan leaned his head back against the couch. "I screwed up. I apologized though and I did take Gracie's advice."

"You did? What did you do?" Lexi didn't try to hide the surprise in her answer.

"C'mon, Lexi, you've seen me work and you can't have forgotten your job. When China calls, we have to answer. I said I was sorry."

"Did you send flowers to Gracie, or do anything to convey your sincere apology?"

Oops. That would have been a good move. Jordan put his hand over his face. "Um, I hired three assistants and I got a dog."

"Wait, what?" Lexi said. "Did you just say you got a dog?"

Jordan smiled. "Yes, she actually saved my life the night of that date. I was about to get mugged and maybe worse. Instead, I found a little black lab puppy."

"Oh, Jordan, you have to send me some pictures. Why haven't you sent me pictures?"

"Maybe because I wasn't sure if I would keep the dog after she chewed up my Santoni shoes."

Lexi gasped. "Oh no, you wouldn't take her back to the streets!"

"Of course not, but I might have thought about taking her back to the animal shelter."

Thankfully, Lexi didn't ask what he meant by taking her back. "Send me pictures. And Jordan?"

"Yes?"

"I'd like you to come see me in Kauai in January and I'm not taking no for answer."

There was a hint of something in her voice, as if she was smiling even as she was commanding him to come visit her. "Why what's going on in January?"

"I'm getting married!"

"Whoa! Really? That's great Lexi. Who's the lucky guy?"

"Jordy! You know it's Derek." Lexi laughed. "I miss you."

He missed his little sister too. Teasing, laughing, and working together had brought him closer to his sister, and left a void when she moved. "I miss you too. So when did Derek propose?"

"Last night. It was on Ke'e beach after we went snorkeling and saw a family of turtles."

"Sounds romantic."

"Like you would know," Lexi teased, "but yes, it was perfect. I'm so happy in love!"

Jordan stood and walked through his spacious kitchen. "I'm really happy for you, Lexi. And I'll definitely be there, even if it means hiring another assistant."

"Let me know if you need help finding a date for the wedding," Lexi teased.

"Hey, I might surprise you," Jordan replied.

"Send me a picture of that puppy!"

"Okay, will do. Love you, Sis."

Right after the call ended, Jordan blew out a breath, rolled his shoulders back and texted Madison: **Hey, want to help me take Roxie on her leash on the Riverwalk?**

Jordan pushed send and then went to check on Roxie. The new doggie door had been installed and she was much happier with her freedom to go out into the backyard. Jordan practiced a few of the commands Madison had taught him and rewarded Roxie with a treat, focusing all of his attention on his puppy, instead of obsessively checking his phone. After at least ten minutes, his phone chimed.

Madison: **That's a great idea! Can you meet tomorrow at five?**

58

Jordan checked his schedule. Tomorrow he would be continuing the training for his assistants and he had several meetings, but his goal was to be done by four-thirty. **How about five-thirty?**

Madison: **I'll be there.**

Okay, it wasn't an actual date but Jordan felt like it was as close as he'd come in the past year.

"He just asked me on a date!" Madison jumped up and down and thrust her phone in front of Sue.

"Uh-oh girl, you in trouble," Sue said with a smile, "but it's the good kind of trouble."

"Do you think so?" Madison looked back at the text. "Maybe it isn't really a date? Oh, this is awkward. What if I just squealed for nothing?"

Sue harrumphed. "It's a date. Busy man ask you to meet him at the Riverwalk after work to train his dog? That's just a excuse to see you."

Madison bit her bottom lip, her finger hovering over the screen. Part of her wished that she could just reply, *So does this count as a date?* Instead she slipped her phone into her pocket and returned to work. She'd just have to wait until tomorrow to see how things went. Sue tugged on her ponytail when she caught her daydreaming.

"Better save some of your dreams with Mr. Billionaire for tonight."

Madison chuckled and swatted Sue's arm. "Okay, okay, I'll try to focus."

But she didn't do a very good job because she kept analyzing her interactions with Jordan up to this point. His green eyes, blond hair, and toned body kept playing through her mind. When she got home she spent almost an hour picking out the perfect outfit that was cute, but still fell within the dog training category. And then she spent extra time putting together some notes for Jordan to use with Roxie. Tomorrow she'd find out if she was just a dog trainer or maybe something a little more.

Chapter 11

The day was full of paperwork and filing for grants for the spay and neuter clinic in downtown Chicago. Madison planned to get off work at two o'clock, but at three-thirty she was barely finishing up with a new check-in. The golden retriever would go fast, but Madison needed to run a few tests first to make sure the dog, who was at least two years old, hadn't been abused. She gave the dog a few extra minutes, trying to infuse love and care into the trembling dog, reassuring him that all would be well.

"I thought you had an appointment with one of your clients to get to," Sue said. "What are you still doing here?" Her salt and pepper hair was pulled back into a tight bun, a few coarse strands coming loose around her ears.

"This one is tugging at my heart," Madison said. "He's shaking."

Sue clucked her tongue. "Poor thing. Let me talk to him and you go on home. I'll see you tomorrow."

Madison stood, keeping her hand on the dog and murmuring softly. "Thanks, Sue."

"You working with that handsome fella and the black lab?" Sue asked with a twinkle in her eye.

"Yes, and Roxie is very smart. I think she does have some border collie in her. She's quite receptive to the little bit of training we've done so far."

"And how about the mister? There isn't a missus, is there?"

Madison shook her finger at Sue. "No. He's a client, that's all." She'd had time to think last night, and decided that it probably didn't count as a date. She didn't want to get her hopes up, even if she had been excited the day before.

Sue shrugged. "Could be more I think."

"Why do you think that?"

"You been acting different is all." Sue sat on a folding chair next to the golden retriever and patted her lap. "Here boy, let's have us a visit. Mr. Burke is a real one. I don't think you'd go wrong paying him some attention."

"You're right, I'd better go now. It's getting late." Madison waved and headed for the door with Sue chuckling behind her.

She hurried to her apartment and changed into walking clothes, taking an extra minute to put in silver hoop earrings and retouch her makeup. *He's my client,* she reminded herself, but that didn't stop her from checking her hair and applying a spritz of her lime citrus perfume.

The Riverwalk was basically in the backyard of Burke Enterprises and hundreds of other businesses in the skyscrapers dotting the city. Chicago continued to make improvements to the Riverwalk so that people all over the world could take in the sights. Madison took the L again and the train was nearly ten minutes late, but when she arrived she didn't see Jordan anywhere. She checked her phone and saw a text indicating that he was on his way. She looked at the sky and walked toward the street. The weather was often unpredictable, especially because of the lake effect, but September generally was an excellent time to stroll along the river.

She was just about to check her watch again when a sleek black Mercedes pulled up and deposited Jordan at the curb. Madison waved at the driver, thinking that she could get used to being chauffeured around.

"Hi, Madison," Jordan said as he stretched his arms overhead. His gray t-shirt looked good with his blond hair. Madison noticed his well-defined biceps as he opened the door, helping Roxie out of her kennel. He looked different in casual clothes. His khaki cargo shorts sent a very different message than the pinstriped suit. *Okay, quit ogling*, Madison chided herself. She focused on Roxie and laughed out loud at the excitement emanating from every part of the puppy. Her entire body wagged along with her tail and she half-jumped several times, receiving a stern warning from Jordan.

"She really is adorable, aren't you, Roxie?" Madison patted Roxie's head and then gave her a few quick commands, rewarded by doggie treats.

"She's been a lot happier since she's had access to the back yard. Of course, my yard is now a war zone with land mines everywhere and I'm sure my gardener is cursing Roxie's spots on the grass."

There was a happy note to Jordan's voice and Madison was again reminded of a little boy, getting the wish of his life in a cherished dog. "I'm glad things are working better. Let's start off with this harness and see how Roxie does. I'm glad you're strong because you're going to need those muscles." As soon as the words were out, Madison's face heated with embarrassment. She'd just openly admitted checking out Jordan's body. She looked over at him, but he didn't seem fazed by her remark. "Okay, let me give you a few pointers first."

Madison guided Roxie along the path, giving commands, and pulling up quick on the leash when Roxie went the wrong direction. Several times, Roxie tried to bound forward and jerked Madison's arm, but she held on tight and pulled back. "Heel, Roxie. Yes. Good girl."

"I think I understand the phrase, 'Keep him on a short leash' much better now," Jordan said.

"I know it seems a bit harsh at first, but Roxie will be much happier once she understands how to work with you. You'll both enjoy the walk so much more." Madison handed the leash to Jordan. "Now, see if you can mimic the way I held the leash. Be firm with her."

Jordan took the leash and Roxie immediately darted forward, her momentum pulling Jordan off balance. Madison couldn't keep from laughing at the sight.

"Hey, I'm not supposed to be entertaining you," Jordan said. "Roxie!" He half-jogged down the path about a hundred yards before he could get Roxie to stop.

Madison hurried to catch up. "Want me to take another turn?"

"Be my guest." Jordan blew out a breath. "This is harder than it looks."

"Really? You make it look so natural," Madison teased.

Jordan rolled his eyes. "It's okay, you can laugh at me. Roxie loves me anyway."

Madison gave the leash a tug and they began walking down the path again. After about five more minutes, Roxie seemed to respond to the lead and she settled into a fast walk beside them. "So you mentioned you have a sister in Kauai. Was it just the two of you growing up?"

"Yep. How about you? Did you just have the one sister?"

"Yes, my parents divorced when Abigail was three, so it was really just my mom and me and my sister."

"That must have been tough," Jordan said.

"It was," Madison replied. "Abigail had a lot of other medical complications that arose as she had more seizures. She needed a lot of treatment and care." There was a lot more to the story than that of course, but Madison didn't want to bring up her father. He had left when he discovered the severity of Abigail's problems and he never came back. He had sent money and taken care of all the medical expenses, but Ben Poplawski wasn't really her father. A father was someone who cared about his family, who had a relationship with his children. The most Ben had ever done was to buy extravagant gifts or deposit more money in her checking account.

"I'm sorry if I brought up bad memories," Jordan said.

Madison looked over at him. How long had she been lost in thought? "No, I'm sorry. How about you? Did you have a good relationship with your parents?"

Jordan's brow furrowed and she saw the pain flash through his eyes even as he opened his mouth to speak. "It was pretty good. Lexi and I were lucky to have such good parents. I just wish we'd had more time with them. I still miss them every day."

"I'm so sorry." Madison put her hand on his arm. "I can't imagine."

"It was such a shock to me and Lexi. We relied on each other a lot after that. Lexi helped get my business to where it is now. She actually just sold her part of the business to me earlier this year."

"It sounds like you two are really close," Madison said.

Jordan tugged on Roxie's leash again. "We are, but I haven't seen her since she moved to Kauai. She just called me last night to tell me that she's getting married."

"Oh that's great! I mean, it is, right?" Madison tilted her head, trying to decipher how Jordan felt.

He sighed. "It is, but I haven't even met the guy. Lexi has invited me out a dozen times, but I was always too busy."

"You trust her though, right? To find a good guy?"

Jordan nodded. "I do, and I've heard nothing but good things about him. I've even talked to him a few times over the phone. I shouldn't be surprised that my little sister is getting married, but I am anyway."

"Does part of you feel sad that her fiancé didn't ask your permission?"

Jordan's lips twitched. "No, not that. I guess it's just hitting me pretty hard that my life is passing by while I've been working my guts out to have a successful company."

"My mom likes to remind me that I can be sad about things or I can do something about it. Are you making some changes in your company so that you can have more freedom?"

"I like that." Jordan smiled. "It stings a bit, but not so much that I can't hear the advice."

Madison's words were perhaps more bold than they should be with this man that she hardly knew, but for a moment she felt like the edges of their souls were touching and that Jordan was opening up to her, maybe in a way he hadn't to anyone in a long time. "I used to hate it when she said that to me as a kid, but now I find myself saying it way more than I should."

"I think I need to listen up because everyone I run into lately keeps giving me the same message: don't work your life away." Jordan pulled back slightly on Roxie's leash as they headed down toward the river. "I don't know how to do anything else though. Ever since my parents died, I've drowned myself in work."

The worried tone in his voice cried out for help and Madison wished that she could put her arms around Jordan and reassure him. She reached out tentatively and took his free hand, squeezing it gently. "I looked into your company. You've done amazing things and provided jobs for people—changed lives—all over the world. Your programs are wonderful. You *are* successful."

Jordan's eyes widened as she took his hand. He hesitated half a second before squeezing her fingers. "Thank you, Madison." He kept holding her hand as they walked along the paved pathway farther away from the heart of the city. There were runners, bicyclists, and people on the river, but for a moment it felt like just the two of them, and of course, the cute puppy tangled up in her leash.

Jordan bent to untangle Roxie and then stood close to Madison. "Hey, can I take you out to dinner sometime?"

The birds seemed to sing louder in the trees as Madison smiled and said, "I would love that."

Jordan grinned. "How about Giordano's deep dish pizza? Are you a fan?"

Immediately, her mouth began watering. "I can almost taste it now."

Jordan chuckled. "Tomorrow at seven?"

"Yes, but let's eat at seven, so you'd better pick me up at six-fifteen."

He pulled his bottom lip between his teeth and then gave one quick nod of his head. "It'll take some work, but I'll be there."

After the walk, Madison gave Jordan her address, and then she rubbed Roxie's belly. "You did a great job, girl. You'll be a pro in no time."

"Thanks, Madison. This was great." Jordan motioned to his driver as he pulled up to the curb.

"Next week at your place. The usual time?" Madison tried to ease the butterflies in her stomach as she thought about the dinner invitation Jordan had extended.

Jordan gave her a thumbs up and then he lifted Roxie into her kennel. The puppy yipped and Jordan paused to rub behind her ears. Madison watched Jordan and didn't try to fight the growing attraction she felt. Jordan's t-shirt fit snugly and the muscles along his back suggested that he didn't just sit in an office chair all day. Jordan was a busy man, but he took care of himself. He turned and Madison smiled, caught staring at him again. It wasn't just his natural good looks, but the way that he interacted with Roxie that caught her attention. Jordan Burke had a lot of love to give, but for some reason he hadn't allowed himself to give it. Madison glanced back one more time before walking away, her heart fluttering as she thought about what it might be like to kiss Jordan.

Chapter 12

*J*ordan attended six meetings, sat in on two conference calls, and at five-thirty, he finally admitted that there was no way he could get through Chicago's traffic to pick up Madison by six-fifteen. He was about to call Madison when he thought of an idea. One of his assistants had strongly encouraged him to hire another driver for employee use so that Jordan's driver would always be free. For the past week, Jordan had been testing out the new hire. The man had come highly recommended and tonight he could save Jordan. With a smile, Jordan made the call, ordering the driver to pick up Madison at six-fifteen. Jordan finished up the details for the next Falzon meeting, and even though it was difficult, he off-loaded a few more things onto his new assistants.

It had been six months since Lexi had left Burke Enterprises. She had personally hired three people to take her place and had tried to convince Jordan to do the same without success. *Lexi is getting married and I'm still working twelve hour days*, Jordan thought. He shook his head. Something had to give, but he didn't know how to make it all happen. He loved his business, the feeling of success, and the money to do whatever he wanted. But he'd never considered that to be successful he would have to give up all of his freedom. Well, tonight would be different. He walked out to Wang's office. His main Chinese liaison worked from four in the afternoon to two in the morning every day. He was in the office during prime work hours for the Burke office in China and he handled all of the problems that came up while the Western world was sleeping.

"Hey, Wang, I have a really important meeting tonight and I can't be interrupted," Jordan said. "I'm going to leave my phone with you. I know you can handle anything that comes up."

Wang nodded. "Yes, sir. And will you be back for your phone?"

Jordan hesitated before answering. "I'll send the driver back for it so that I can have it after the meeting. Sound good?"

"Yes, very good."

Jordan smiled and patted Wang on the back. "Thank you."

Feeling lighter than he had in five years, Jordan headed to his private bathroom, showered, and changed into a clean button up shirt, but he skipped the tie. Tonight he was living life on his own terms, and he couldn't wait to see Madison.

Madison had been surprised when a man knocked on her door and handed her a card from Burke Enterprises. At first she was afraid that Jordan was canceling their date, but he'd sent a driver in a fancy silver car to pick her up. The hood ornament looked like another Mercedes, but Madison had never really been into cars. Of course, once she sat in the soft leather seats and glided along through rush hour traffic, she decided that maybe luxury cars were something to put on her wish list.

When she entered Giordano's, the aroma of fresh basil, warm spaghetti sauce, and spicy pepperoni tickled her nose. Her stomach roared to life and Madison looked for Jordan, hoping he wouldn't be late. Remembering what he'd said about his last date, Madison was prepared to order and eat by herself because there was no way she could walk away from the divine smells of melted cheese and homemade pizza crust. She approached the hostess, but had only taken two steps when she felt a hand on her arm.

"Did I keep you waiting long?"

Madison turned and sucked in a breath. Jordan looked...delicious. His light green eyes crinkled at the edges with his smile and when he gave her arm a light squeeze, Madison forgot all about pizza. He wore a light orange dress shirt with tan pants and as she stepped closer, she caught the woodsy scent that she recognized as his cologne. "You're right on time. I was just thinking that if you didn't get here soon, I'd have to eat without you."

Jordan put a hand over his heart. "I promise to do better tonight."

"Well, then, let's get to it," Madison replied.

Once they were seated, Jordan ordered a traditional Chicago style deep-dish pizza and a side of cheesy garlic breadsticks. The waitress brought out three kinds of dipping sauce. Madison tried the balsamic vinaigrette with undertones of garlic and groaned. "This is so good."

"Mm, hmm," Jordan murmured around a mouthful of steaming bread. "I need to do this more often."

"Do you have a personal chef?" Madison asked.

Jordan nodded. "I have a full staff for my home, but I probably don't enjoy it as much as I should. At least that's what my sister tells me."

"So a full staff? Is that like a maid and a gardener, or what?" Madison dipped her breadstick in the sauce and took another bite.

Jordan finished chewing his breadstick and smiled. "I hope this doesn't make you think less of me, but yes I have a gardener, a chef, a maid, a driver, and several personal assistants."

Madison raised her eyebrows. "I had no idea. It's hard to fathom the amount of work you must do to be a billionaire."

Jordan shrugged. "I've always been kind of a workaholic, and it seems like most of the people in my life have spent a lot of time telling me not to be."

Madison chewed her breadstick thoughtfully, unsure of how to answer to Jordan's last remark. There was definitely a note of bitterness or possibly grief in his words. "You mentioned that Lexi would like you to come and visit her. And you told me you hired some new assistants. Do you love your work, or do you hope to retire at a young age?"

"I used to think that I'd retire in my thirties back when I was in my twenties. But now I'm not sure how to make it happen. I don't know, it just seems like every year things get busier and busier." A phone dinged at the table next to them and Jordan reached for his pocket, shook his head, and then smiled at Madison.

"Well how do other billionaires do it?" Madison asked. "It seems to me like they must've figured something out to be flying all over the world, owning private islands and lounging in the sun."

Jordan laughed. "That's just the side the media wants to see. Showing how hard someone really works would be boring. I'm sure all those people have fought the same battles that I do."

"Well, it sounds like it's a worthy battle to fight. If you don't have freedom, what do you have?"

"Thank goodness, there's our pizza."

Madison looked up as the server brought out the steaming pizza in the deep dish to their table. Her stomach growled and she let the abrupt change in the subject happen. She'd obviously touched near one of Jordan's tender spots. It did make her curious though, why that spot was so tender.

"So, what are your plans?" Jordan asked as he helped dish up the pizza. "Are you hoping to have enough clients to train dogs full-time or do you enjoy working at the animal shelter?"

"Well, I'm starting to think more seriously about starting my own business."

"Really?" Jordan leaned forward, his face open and eager. "What kind of business?"

"Nothing as big as yours, but I do want to make a difference and keep working with animals."

Madison didn't wait for Jordan to reply. She took a bite of pizza and concentrated on the taste of thick pizza sauce coating the perfectly spicy pepperoni. She was preparing herself for this conversation because the last time she'd told a guy about her dreams, he'd stomped on them pretty fast.

"Are you being intentionally vague or am I supposed to guess?"

"Maybe both?" Madison took another bite of pizza and tried not to smile at the bewildered look on Jordan's face.

"I can play this game too." He took a large bite of pizza and pointed his fork at Madison. "What kind of business—the one you mentioned about working with dogs?"

Madison wiped her mouth with a napkin. "Yes, I want to set up a center for service dog training. There are dozens of different kinds of service dogs and I've been in training for the past few years, learning some special techniques. Eventually, I'd like to teach others how to train the dogs."

"Wow, that sounds really cool. So what's your next move? How close are you to starting this business?"

He was listening and Madison leaned forward, excitement building in her chest. "People usually discourage me from my dream."

"Then you must be talking to the wrong people." Jordan held a bite in front of his mouth and winked at her. "If a college dropout like me can start Burke Enterprises, you can follow your dreams."

"Thank you," Madison replied. If she could have hugged Jordan right then without making a scene and smearing pizza sauce across his orange shirt, she totally would.

"So not like seeing eye dogs, but a different kind of service dog?" Jordan asked.

"Exactly. I want to train service dogs for specific needs. For example, did you know that there are service dogs who sleep with diabetics because they can smell their breath and know when their blood sugar drops too low?"

"Wow, that's amazing. I've never heard of anything like it." Jordan pulled his breadstick apart and dunked it the dipping sauce.

"It is fascinating. My friend hadn't slept through the night in years because her daughter is diabetic and nighttime is one of the most dangerous times for blood sugar to drop. When they got their service dog it changed her life. She said she feels like a different person now."

"I can see why you want to do something like that."

"Yes, because I want to make a difference in people's lives." Madison took another bite of pizza. She didn't want to get carried away and say too much about her business, but it was hard to resist with how receptive Jordan was to her ideas. Usually people didn't understand what she meant about service dog training, or they didn't think it was worth all the time that a person would have to invest. Jordan hadn't discounted any of her ideas; in fact he seemed genuinely interested.

"I think you should go for it, Madison. What's stopping you?"

She gripped her fork, trying to think how to answer his question. "I guess I never had much encouragement and it's a scary thing to do on your own. It's a huge investment and not something you can do halfway."

"Well if anyone can do it, it's you. I've seen you work. Go for it."

Madison felt like Jordan had just turned on a light in her soul. She studied his face. He believed in her, and she needed that. "I can tell you like animals too," Madison said. "Maybe that's why you understand why this is so important to me."

Jordan looked down at his plate. "I just think that if you have a dream that compels you, you shouldn't let anyone tell you that you can't do it."

Madison reached across the table and put her hand over Jordan's. "Thank you. That's what I needed to hear today."

He turned his hand over and clasped hers. "I meant every word."

"You have a little pizza on your shirt." Madison pointed to the spot of red sauce on his orange shirt.

"Oh, man. This pizza was just too good." He grabbed a napkin, dipped it in his water and dabbed at the spot on his shirt. He really was just a normal guy, and as Madison watched him scrub at his shirt, little napkin fibers dotting the fine fabric, she was reminded at how young he was. Being a billionaire was an incredible accomplishment, but was Jordan's success at the expense of the rest of his life? He hadn't liked her questions earlier so she decided to keep to lighter topics, but she must tread carefully with her heart.

Chapter 13

The following week was a nightmare for Burke Enterprises. Jordan was so busy that he had to cancel his training session with Madison and Roxie. He could hear the disappointment in her voice but there was nothing he could do. They were looking at breaking a new set of records for the quarter and Jordan felt a pressure on his shoulders that never seemed to ease. He thought about the fight that he had had with his dad again.

Cecil Burke had always hoped for great things for his children and because Jordan had always been attached to animals, being a veterinarian seemed like the natural course. When Jordan was young he had embraced the idea and continued to get good grades in school. It looked like vet school could be a possibility. But after his first year of college, Jordan dropped out, deciding that wasn't the course he wanted after all. It crushed his father's dreams of his son being a successful veterinarian. At least that's the way Jordan had always seen it, that his father wouldn't have bragging rights for him. But now Jordan wondered. He thought about that last conversation that he had with his father. His dad had asked him, "Are you happy? Do you really want to give up on college?"

At the time Burke Enterprises didn't exist. Jordan was hustling doing a side business that would later turn into his billion-dollar business while working part-time.

Jordan shrugged off the memory and leaned over his desk. Work was the only thing that could keep the questions at bay.

Even though he was busier than he wanted to be and work was his top priority, Jordan couldn't stop thinking about Madison. The way her eyes sparkled when she laughed and the dark curls that framed her face. Every time he was around her, he felt relaxed in a way that he never could create on his own. He loved working with her and Roxie and sometimes he thought that maybe he could have a different life—until his schedule started beeping at him with another appointment reminder.

He had just finished another conference call and leaned back in his chair, swiveling to see the view of Chicago out his office window. The city was an architectural masterpiece with buildings of every color and design. When he first designed his office he planned to spend several minutes each day looking out the window and taking in the wonder around him. Jordan realized that now weeks passed without him really noticing his surroundings. It was time to change all that. He'd started making strides to change—adopting Roxie had definitely created an upheaval in his busy life. Then there was Madison. He definitely wanted to spend more time with her.

The other night when they'd gone to the pizza place, he'd left his phone behind and everything was fine. His staff had handled everything and he'd been able to enjoy Madison's presence. Her laughter, witty remarks, and kind curiosity had been exactly what he needed.

Jordan pushed the button on the console and got Porter on the phone.

"Hey, I need two tickets for a riverboat cruise. While you're at it, can you help me figure out how to make it more romantic?"

Porter laughed. "Dude, we need to get you into training. I'll buy all the tickets for the next tour. How about Saturday morning for romance training? Would that work?"

Jordan tapped his desk twice and smiled. "That's a great idea. I'll get right back with you with the final answer."

Jordan's fingers trembled as he texted Madison to ask her on a date Saturday down the Chicago River. He felt like a kid in high school, and in some ways he still was because he never dated enough to have much experience. A few minutes later, Jordan pumped his fist in the air as he read Madison's reply: **Yes, I'd love to!**

Saturday morning, Madison said she would take the L to meet Jordan at the riverboat cruise even though he offered the services of his driver. He liked how genuine she was—so different from some of the women he'd dated who were obviously enamored with his money. Madison was independent and courageous enough to be herself, and Jordan was falling hard for her.

When they met up, Madison smiled and Jordan forgot why he was so worried about the date. They'd been aboard the boat for a few minutes before Madison gave him a curious look. "Did you charter this boat just for us?"

Jordan grinned. "I might have had a little help with that, but yes, it's just you, me, and the crew."

Madison looped her arm through his. "That is so neat! Thank you, Jordan."

The way she beamed up at him made Jordan want to buy the whole boat if it would get her to smile that carefree way again. He put his arm around her and they walked to the railing. "I can't remember the last time I did something that qualifies as a tourist attraction in this city."

"Ditto," Madison replied. "There is so much to see here and we're stuck working while people all over the country come to see the sights."

"We should do something about that, huh?"

"Should we?"

Jordan nodded. He wasn't sure what they could do about it since he was so busy that this was the first time in the past two years he had even taken anyone on a second date, but he was here today with Madison. And something felt different, there was a possibility that maybe he could change—that life would allow him to change.

"You must have a lot on your mind." Madison jolted him from his thoughts.

"What? Oh, yeah," Jordan said. "Just thinking that it feels good to do something fun once in a while."

Madison leaned against the railing—absent of any other tourists. The boat was quiet as they traveled through the heart of the city. She turned to look at him. "How many hours a week do you usually work?"

"Ugh, you don't want to know." Jordan tried to sidestep the question.

"No, really, I want to know. So tell me." Madison gripped the railing and gave him a look that said, *You're not changing the subject on me this time.*

"I've shaved off a few hours the past couple weeks." Jordan wiped a hand over his face. "Usually sixty to seventy, but I'm working on that."

"You're *working* on that?" Madison stood upright. "That's the problem. You're working on everything. Jordan, you're going to kill yourself if you keep that up. How long have you been putting in those kinds of hours?"

"Most of the past four years." Jordan grimaced. "Please don't give me a lecture. I get that enough from my sister."

Madison held up her hand. "Okay, I won't waste my breath if you can answer one question."

"Shoot."

"Why?"

Jordan scrunched his eyebrows together. "Why what?"

"Why are you working so hard? And don't give me some trite answer. Tell me the real reason because there's one underneath that armor." She poked him in the chest.

Jordan grabbed her hand and covered it with both of his. "Isn't there another question I could answer, like what's the price of tea in China?"

Madison giggled and pulled her hand free so that she could shake her finger at him. "You agreed."

"Technically, I said 'shoot' and what I meant was, Shoot, the guide is about to start telling us about this building right here." And right on cue, the tour guide did start into his program about the buildings edging the river.

"Okay, I'll give you a delay, but you're not getting out of this." Madison folded her arms and stared at the Hancock Building that the guide was talking about. The 100 story building rose up into the sky and the guide explained that nearly half of the building was residential.

Jordan smiled and put his arm around Madison, pulling her close to his side. Her nearness made it hard to pay attention to the random facts coming from the speaker above their heads. Hopefully he could distract Madison from her question because if he was being truthful, he didn't know how to answer it.

Their time together sped by too quickly, and Madison was grateful that they could talk freely without worrying about anyone or anything else. By the time they reached the end of the riverboat cruise, Madison had snuggled up to Jordan to shield herself from the wind coming off the water. The weather had changed abruptly when the sun hid behind the clouds and a cool September breeze decided to dance through the changing leaves of the maple trees nearby. Her hand was warm though because

Jordan held it, his fingers interlaced with hers. She noticed the fancy watch on his wrist and remembered that he was a billionaire. He was so unlike her father, she kept forgetting to be cautious of him. *Be careful*, the familiar warning chanted *he can hurt you just like Dad did*. But Jordan hadn't done or said anything to flaunt his wealth or make her feel uncomfortable. If anything, his workaholic status made it easy to forget that he was a billionaire. Madison chose to ignore the scare tactics that her memories were playing on her.

Jordan was different. He was real and if she'd learned anything from her time with him, Jordan was battling hurts of his own. She couldn't figure out what those hurts were, but with time, perhaps he would open up. The first day she'd met him, she'd sensed that he carried a scar from the loss of his childhood dog, but Jordan had never mentioned the particulars. As she thought back to that day, she wondered if his dog hadn't been gone as long as she originally thought. It was obvious that adopting Roxie had been a difficult step forward on his path to healing.

"It feels different not having Roxie here, doesn't it?" Madison said softly.

"Yeah, I was thinking the same thing. She definitely makes every situation a bit more chaotic."

"How are things going between you two?"

"Well, she's been sleeping better at night, which is good because I definitely don't want her licking my face in the middle of the night."

Madison started laughing and Jordan gave her a puzzled look. "What? What's so funny?"

She laughed harder and waved her free hand at Jordan. "I was thinking how our conversation would sound to someone else." Jordan arched an eyebrow and then let out a burst of laughter. If someone were to eavesdrop on their conversation, they might think that Madison was asking about Jordan's girlfriend. He pulled her close to him and wrapped his arms around her. "I love the sound of your laugh," he murmured.

Madison swallowed back a girlie squeal and hugged him. "Thank you for giving me a reason to laugh."

Having his arms around her was a feeling Madison could get used to. Her temperature must have raised a few notches because her face felt flushed and the crisp wind felt good on the back of her neck as it picked up the curls and pushed them every which way.

"I'm glad we could do this today." Jordan stepped back from their hug and took her hand again. They walked together off the riverboat cruise and onto the paved path that met up with the Riverwalk.

"It was pretty spectacular having the boat all to ourselves," Madison said.

"It was a first for me." Jordan's cell phone beeped. He checked the message and quickly responded, tucking the phone back into his pocket. "Hey, I have some stuff I need to finish up at the office, but first we should grab a bite to eat."

"Wait, you're going to the office on Saturday?" Madison put a hand on her hip. "What about Roxie?"

"My gardener is bringing his kids over today and they're going to play with her."

"But still, what is so important that you have to work on Saturday? I thought China was a day ahead of us, so isn't it Sunday over there?"

"They don't really take a weekend the way we do," Jordan said.

Madison walked a few paces ahead and stared into the river. "That's sad."

"It is sad, but at the same time it isn't because the people who work in the factories need the money to support their families."

She thought about that for a moment and then looked up at Jordan. "What would happen if you didn't go in to work today?"

He opened his mouth and then closed it. "My inbox is always full. There's always work to do. If I don't go in today, I'll be farther behind on Monday."

"Then you don't have enough employees. Seriously, Jordan, what will you do today that one of your employees couldn't?"

"Hey, aren't you hungry? Let's go to the park and get a chili dog." Jordan tugged on her arm and steered her down the walkway.

Madison shook her head. "You promised that you would answer one question and you didn't. So now I've asked you another. Pick one, but you need to keep your promise."

Jordan groaned. "Do we have to do this now?"

She folded her arms and squared off in front of him. "I'm not moving from this space until I get an answer."

"Okay, okay." He reached out and lightly pushed her shoulder.

"Hey!" Madison took a step back and they both started laughing. "No, you're not getting out of this just because you can make me laugh. Pick a question."

"What were they again?"

Madison narrowed her eyes and Jordan held up his hands. "You got me. I'm not exactly sure of all the work that I would be doing today because so much comes in overnight and I've been busy with my date so I haven't checked my email."

"Not an answer." Madison wasn't going to give him any leeway. She had known which question he would pick and so she tucked away the Why question for later. It was important that she get Jordan to answer that question, no matter how much they both wanted to run away from it.

Jordan's shoulders slumped. "Nothing."

"What?"

"I said, nothing. There's nothing that I would do today that one of my employees couldn't do, hopefully."

Madison took hold of Jordan's hand and squeezed it. "Then don't go. Please? This is the first day off I've had in a long time and I don't want to cut it short."

He looked at their hands and then at her, his head tilting to one side. She wished she could read the thoughts spiraling through his head, the internal argument he was surely having for why he needed to go to work.

"When was the last time you took a Saturday off?" The moment she asked the question, she knew she had him. Jordan's eyes trailed across her face and upwards as he tried to think.

He blew out a breath. "You do understand that I'm the owner of Burke Enterprises, right?"

"I do, and I respect that," Madison replied. "But you're the owner, not the slave, right?"

"You're killing me. What do you want to do?"

Madison threw her arms around his neck. "I want to spend more time with you. Let's start by getting that chili dog."

Chapter 14

Two bites into the chili dog loaded with sour cream and onions and Jordan felt sure that someone would arrest him. He was an escaped convict at one o'clock in the afternoon on a Saturday. Maybe he'd suffer from some sort of brain overload or his skin would catch fire from being exposed to natural sunlight. Even as he had those thoughts, he couldn't keep his eyes off Madison. She was his jail breaker and every moment he spent away from the office gave him more clarity, a sense that maybe Lexi had been right. And a thought that made the back of his throat ache—his father might have been right in his own way.

It had taken him about ten minutes to make the calls needed before Porter told him to quit worrying and let people do their job. Madison had cheered and her laughter rang through the park as they settled in to eat their chili dogs. She squeezed his arm. "You're gonna be okay, you know."

He looked at his watch, the gold-plated face glinting in the sunlight. "I don't know what we're going to do though."

Madison waggled her eyebrows at him. "I have an idea. How late can you stay out?"

Jordan snorted. "I won't be working, so who knows?"

Madison put her hand on his knee. "The Bulls are playing tonight. We could go back to my place and watch it with nachos."

"Basketball?" Jordan couldn't be that lucky. Madison was fantastic, but if she liked basketball too, he was in serious trouble. "You're into the Chicago Bulls?"

"I love a good basketball game."

Jordan put his arm around Madison and pulled her close. "You could've saved yourself a lot of trouble if you would've mentioned that earlier. I wouldn't have had to answer any questions either."

Madison giggled. "So you want to watch the game?"

Jordan had many opportunities to be thankful for his company's success, but in about five seconds, he figured he might be more grateful than he had been in a while. "Yes, but no offense, if I'm going to watch a Bulls game, it's not going to be on any kind of screen."

Madison scrunched up her nose. "What do you mean?"

"My company has box seats."

Madison sat up straight. "You have box seats to the Chicago Bulls!"

"Yep, for the past three years. It was one of my first big splurges." Jordan didn't tell her that he hadn't made it to a game this season and last year he only went to one and that was because Lexi insisted that he meet a client there. When did his life get so out of control that he couldn't even enjoy a basketball game?

"Will the seats still be available this late in the day?"

"Yes, they don't give away my tickets until two hours before game time." Jordan cringed inwardly, thinking that thirty minutes ago he was planning to give up his tickets yet again.

"Oh my goodness! Am I going to go to an actual Chicago Bulls basketball game?"

"Yes, and you're going to be sitting in one of the best seats in the house."

Madison squealed and hugged him. "This is going to be the best date ever."

"I agree." Jordan held her for a minute, loving the fruity scent of her hair. Peaches or apricots? He laughed inwardly. He was smelling a woman's hair and going to a Bulls game. Yep, that sounded like trouble.

They walked through the park, talking about their childhoods, reminiscing over funny stories and holding hands.

"We had so many dogs growing up," Madison said. "My mom took in strays and sometimes they stayed, other times they didn't. I think one of my favorites was a St. Bernard. We named him Tiny."

Jordan laughed. "That reminds me of my boxer, Ralph. I should have named him Tornado or Jet or something. He never sat still for the first five years of his life." Jordan's heart clenched as the memories involving Ralph threatened to overtake him. The words had just flowed out of him unexpectedly. He braced himself for the ache that always accompanied any mention of Ralph, but all he saw was Madison's smile. It faltered as she studied him.

"Ralph was the one—the dog you grew up with?"

Jordan nodded. "I got him when I was twelve. He was the tiniest little pup, and he was always there for me."

"Tiny was only with us for a few years, but I still remember the way he would rest his head on my lap when I watched TV. He always seemed to know when I needed a little extra attention."

Jordan concentrated on her words, leading him carefully away from the hurt over Ralph's loss. Madison hadn't asked for more details, but he knew without asking that she could sense the depth of his feelings surrounding his dog. He was grateful because he wasn't sure how to explain all the emotions that bubbled up every time he thought of the night that Ralph had died. The same night that his parents had died. "You're good for me."

Madison stopped talking, and licked her lips. "I am?"

Her innocence and the way her lips pouted in the middle had his heart pounding. He wanted to kiss her. Did she want him to kiss her? He didn't want to mess this up, especially not in the middle of the park with people everywhere and street vendors calling out. "Yes, you do something to me right here." He pointed at his heart and Madison let out a little sigh.

That must have been romantic. He'd done something right on this date, because the way Madison was looking at him almost gave him the confidence to kiss her right there. Romance. He needed something to show Madison how much she meant to him. He reached out his hand. "We'll have dinner in the box before the game, so we have a little time to kill first. I have an idea. Is it okay if I surprise you?"

She took his hand and her eyes lit up. "A surprise?" Uncertainty crossed her features and she chewed on her bottom lip. "This date has been marvelous, Jordan. I don't want you to feel like you have to do more. The fact that you decided to stay out of the office and spend time with me is a pretty great surprise, wouldn't you agree?"

Jordan chuckled. "I'm still surprised, to be honest. That's why I want this day to be special. Something for the memory books." He pressed his fingers against hers, trying to read the expression on her face. He wasn't an expert at reading body language, but she almost seemed wary. He couldn't figure out why.

She nodded. "Something for the memory books. I'm up for whatever you have planned."

"Now that's putting the pressure on since I'm kind of planning this moment to moment."

Madison patted his arm. "I have confidence in you *and* your assistants."

"Hey, once upon a time I did everything for myself I'll have you know."

"I believe it and I also believe that it's okay for you to admit that you're one man and you can't do everything no matter how much you want to."

There it was again. It was just a light touch of a reminder, but Madison was letting him know that she was serious about him not working so hard. Time for another subject change. "OK, let's go. Prepare to be surprised."

Jordan called his driver and they walked out of the park to the nearest pickup zone. Before Madison got in the car, Jordan gave instructions to his driver for another little surprise stop.

Madison gave him a curious look as he helped her into the car, but Jordan just grinned.

"This will be a short ride, but there's one more place we can't miss before the game." Jordan took her hand and interlaced their fingers.

She gave his hand a squeeze. "I'm all yours today."

Those words had him looking at her mouth again, feeling more confident by the minute that she needed to be kissed today. When the driver pulled to a stop, Jordan helped Madison out of the car and they walked down the sidewalk about a block and a half before stopping in front of a store plastered with Chicago Bulls merchandise. "I'd like to change before the game, but I don't have the right clothes at the office. We should definitely be matching fans, what do you think?"

Madison looked inside the store and then down at her jeans and silky blouse. She smiled. "I'm okay with that."

Jordan took her hand and led her inside the store. "Why don't you pick out your favorite and I'll match you?"

"Okay." Madison was a bit hesitant but then she found a white v-neck shirt with the Bulls logo on it. "This will go great with my jeans. What do you think?"

"You'll look great in that. Now help me find something." Madison put her hand on his arm and guided him to a rack with white t-shirts with a simple design featuring the team logo. She grabbed one and held it up to him.

"I think you might need a jacket to go with it, though."

Jordan snapped his fingers. "Excellent idea. Let's get matching jackets too."

"Oh, you don't need to do that. I'm fine with the shirt."

He bent closer to her. "Hey, let me do this for you, okay? I don't want you to worry about anything. Let's just have fun and enjoy the game like true fans."

The corner of her mouth twitched and Jordan couldn't resist touching her chin, tipping her face upwards. "You're really cute when you do that, you know."

Madison blushed and she looked down, her thick lashes framing those gorgeous eyes of hers—brown with gold and green flecks that drew him in. "Thank you," she murmured.

He rested his hand on the small of her back as they looked at jackets. It was hard to concentrate on anything else except Madison. Every look she gave him pulled his heart closer to hers. She had a perky little mouth that he wanted to kiss, but he couldn't be sure if she would welcome the kiss or not. He was testing the waters by touching her face, her arms, her back, and putting his arm around her. If he didn't mess things up, there would be a goodnight kiss after the most perfect day he'd had in a long time.

The cashier looked very pleased as he rung up the pile of merchandise Jordan had stacked on the counter. He'd talked Madison into getting matching jackets, hats, gloves, water bottles, key chains, and blankets. But the best part was when he found a section for dogs. "Roxie is going to be the biggest Bulls fan in Chicago," Jordan said as he grabbed a dog sweater, leash, and doggie mat in the bold red and black colors of the Bulls.

Madison giggled. "You're out of control, you know."

Jordan shook his head. "I'm the most controlled person I know." It was only after he spoke the words that he heard the irony in them. He *was* controlled. He hadn't felt this free in years and he was starting to get a taste for what Lexi had been telling him the past six months.

"I'm so excited for the game!" Madison said as they carried their bags out of the store. They had changed into their matching shirts and jackets and at the last minute, Jordan had grabbed a duffel bag to keep some of their gear in. His driver picked them up in the black Mercedes down the street and drove them to the stadium. Jordan put his arm around Madison and ran his fingers down her arm.

"This has been a really fun day. Thanks for encouraging me to take a day off."

Madison turned toward him and he could have sworn that her eyes flicked to his mouth before she made eye contact. "It's been a perfect day."

"Can I take you out again sometime?" He took hold of her hand. "Please?"

"Only because you asked so nicely." Madison grinned.

It was a little out of order to ask the girl on a date before their date had ended, but Jordan wanted to make sure that Madison knew how much he enjoyed her company. They were approaching the stadium and he almost wished that they'd got caught in traffic because he wanted to hold Madison close to him, drink in her closeness, and kiss her beautiful lips.

# **Chapter 15**

*J*ust before they exited the car, Madison could've sworn that Jordan wanted to kiss her and she would've let him. The chemistry between them was tangible and she found that she didn't want to lose contact with him. The way he held her hand, touched her cheek, or pulled her in close to his side told her that he was feeling the same connection.

Jordan took her around the east side of the United Stadium to show her a statue of Michael Jordan going up for a slam dunk. They talked about watching the legend as kids and how Jordan made basketball come alive for them.

"I can't believe I'm really going to see the Bulls play!" Madison couldn't contain her excitement.

Jordan put his arm around her and pulled her in for a hug. "Thanks for coming with me."

They stepped inside the glass doors of the stadium and Jordan reached over and tucked a strand of hair behind her ear. *If my heart beats any harder, he's going to hear it.* Madison smiled and stood close to him as they looked around the stadium. Huge screens hung over the basketball court and Madison noticed the section of box seats where large corporate offices like Burke Enterprises would watch the game tonight—where she would watch the game tonight. The smell of cinnamon almonds reminded Madison of Christmas time and she turned to see the nut stand a few feet away. "Those smell so good."

"I know," Jordan replied. "We're definitely getting a bag." He tugged on her hand and they walked toward the vendor. A moment later, Madison held a warm sack of delectable almonds cooked in sugar and cinnamon. Jordan shoved a handful in his mouth and closed his eyes. "Yep, they are as good as they smell."

Madison took a ladylike handful and the flavor burst in her mouth as she crunched the nuts. It didn't seem like it had been that long since they'd enjoyed a chili dog in the park but it was almost six-thirty and Madison's stomach was tugging at her brain again.

"You're going to love the buffet. We got a new catering company this year and they always do a great job."

"How do you know?" Madison asked. "I bet you haven't even been to a game this year."

Jordan touched the tip of her nose. "Delivery. That's how. My assistants always find a way to feed me when I'm working late on a game night."

"I bet it'll taste even better tonight then." Madison walked alongside Jordan as he led her up an escalator and toward the box seats in the stadium. How could a man like Jordan work so hard that he missed something he obviously loved so much week after week? The niggling thought picked at her happiness, but Madison pushed it aside. Maybe Jordan just needed a reason to change. *He's not like my dad, he's different*, she told herself. Jordan had worked hard to create a successful company and it was easy to see how hard it would be to transition from the man who did everything to the man who let other people do everything and directed it all. He was trying, so Madison was willing to give him a chance.

They stepped inside the box and Madison admired the great view of the game floor. There were plush leather seats lined up in the front of the box and a buffet table along the back.

"Our seats are over here." Jordan led her to the very front row with two seats marked VIP. Several people greeted Jordan with thanks for the seats and excitement over the game as they walked by. Based on the number of seats, the box was about half-full, but once everyone came there would be about twenty people in the Burke Enterprises box. Madison had grown up watching the Bulls games on their old TV, cheering alongside Abigail.

"I wish Abigail could have experienced something like this," Madison said softly. "She would have loved it."

Jordan pursed his lips. "It's not fair, is it?"

Madison shook her head, the loss settling on her heart once again. Jordan touched her cheek. "I don't think she would want you to be sad."

She put her hand over his. "You're right. In fact, she'd be ticked if I wasn't up there screaming my guts out for the win."

99

He pulled her toward the buffet. "Same goes for good food, right?"

She took a plate and then caught sight of the dessert table. "Is that cherry chocolate cheesecake?"

Jordan looked over her head and grinned. "My favorite, and it's the Bulls colors so that means I can have two slices."

"I'd better eat my salad first so it can cancel out the calories." Madison scooped up a hefty serving of the Caesar salad and moved toward a server who placed a grilled chicken breast on her plate. "Thank you. This looks delicious."

They talked to a few other business executives from Burke Enterprises, and for a moment it looked like Jordan might get caught up in some sort of issue. He pulled out his phone, started texting, and then looked over at Madison. A muscle ticked in his jaw as he tilted the phone back and forth and then pocketed it, holding up his hand to stop the other executive from continuing.

"We'll figure it out later," Jordan said as he guided Madison to a table for two set up near the VIP seating. She felt a thrill at the determined look on Jordan's face. He had made a choice for her and it quieted all the worries she'd been entertaining each time she felt herself falling for Jordan. She was falling hard now.

Madison wanted to devour her food, but she forced herself to take small bites so she could talk to Jordan without a full mouth. As the day had progressed, it seemed that Jordan relaxed a bit more and Madison started to see a carefree side of him that she imagined might have been more dominant in his younger days. By the time the basketball game started, Madison was convinced that if Jordan had enough opportunities, he might remember how important it was to have fun.

The game started off with Jake McConnell stealing the ball and dunking it. The crowd never did come down after that.

Madison and Jordan cheered, screamed, and booed when needed. They gave each other high fives and the intensity of the game made everything about Jordan seem more real. When he put his hand on Madison's back, she could feel the way his large palm covered the space and made her feel safe. In the final minute of the game, McConnell shot a huge three to take the lead and was fouled. The crowd went crazy. Madison and Jordan jumped up and he pulled her into a hug, whooping as he spun her around. Laughter bubbled up inside her and she tipped her head back and smiled as Jordan pulled her close. Her face was right next to his and Jordan looked so happy in that moment, his green eyes lighting up, that Madison wished she could take a picture and show him later to prove to them both that he was the same man.

"Having fun?" Madison said with a wink. "Thinking about doing this more often?"

Jordan nodded and then he leaned in and kissed her. The moment his lips touched hers, fire ignited in her soul. Madison put her hands on his chest, almost forgetting that they were standing in the VIP section of the box seats. It was just Jordan and her, and she didn't want the moment to end. She smiled and before she could say anything, Jordan kissed her again. It was only a light peck, but Madison felt the kiss all the way to her toes, a spark threading through every one of her nerves.

"I need you," he whispered.

"I'm right here," she said. The moment was already etching itself into an unforgettable memory—her first kiss with Jordan at a Chicago Bulls game.

Jordan pulled her close as the buzzer sounded, ending the game with a win for the Chicago Bulls. Madison touched her lips, feeling the spark from Jordan and hoping for more.

The stadium erupted into celebratory cheers that continued as Madison and Jordan exited the building. The night had cooled and the Windy City was practicing its namesake with icy gusts that had Jordan and Madison jogging to the curbside to be picked up by his driver. The heated seats felt like a gift as Madison settled in next to Jordan. He put his arm around her and pulled her close. They hadn't talked much since Jordan had spoken the words that penetrated Madison's heart. *I need you.* She wanted him to need her, but at the same time she was afraid of needing him too much.

"Hey, Maddie. Can I call you Maddie?" Jordan asked.

"Sure, does that mean I should call you Jordy?"

He rolled his eyes. "Lexi has called me Jordy forever, but I only tolerate that one."

Madison laughed, remembering the first time she'd met Jordan on the streets of Chicago while she walked two dogs—one named Jordy. "Maybe we'll have to think of a new one then."

"Or not. I had a great time tonight."

"Me too."

Jordan pulled his bottom lip through his teeth and Madison could barely keep herself from leaning forward and kissing him again. He gave her a strained smile.

"What's wrong?"

He lifted a shoulder and let it fall. "I'm just worried about how I'll recreate this again. I've really been trying to lighten my load but if you could see my schedule for this coming week, I think you'd be afraid."

"What are you saying?" Madison tried to read between the lines, but Jordan wasn't an easy book to read.

"I'm saying that I want to spend time with you, but this is new to me."

"Oh, you mean acting like a normal person and taking a day off?" Madison infused a lightness to her tone that hid the turmoil underneath. Jordan was touching the hotplate of her worries and alarms were going off everywhere in her head.

"Yes, that's exactly what I mean. I have another trip to China coming up in three weeks and I'll be gone for ten days. I used to love going but now it's just exhausting."

"Is there a way that you can have someone go in your place?" Madison placed her hand on his and she loved the way that he flipped his palm up and interlaced their fingers.

He blew out a breath. "I don't know. I've always been the one to go. I'm familiar with every aspect of our factories over there and I speak Chinese. That's a requirement that clears out a lot of people."

"I'm sure if it's important enough to you, you'll find a way to make it work. You're a smart and successful guy. You didn't get to this place without hard work, but it also took a lot of creativity and ingenuity. Am I right?"

Jordan wrinkled his brow. She could almost see him processing the idea she had presented. *You can do this!* she wanted to shout, but she kept quiet, giving him space to think. He nodded slowly. "Yes, you're right."

He leaned forward and kissed her temple. "Thanks for being patient with me."

The kiss was nice, but what did that mean? Was he going to try to reduce his workload? He'd made some great strides in just the past few weeks so Madison bit back the words of advice she wanted to press on him. Instead, she sat a little closer to him and enjoyed the feel of his arm around her. When the driver pulled up to her apartment, Jordan walked her inside.

"Would you like to come in for a minute?"

"Sure, I'd like to see your place." Jordan waited while she unlocked the door and they stepped inside.

She loved her little apartment but as they stepped inside, she saw it through his eyes. The sofa was worn and the braided multi-colored rug on the hardwood floor was clean but frayed on the edges. Before she could excuse how tiny her apartment was compared to his home, Jordan smiled. "I can tell this is your place. It looks great. It's like you."

"Thank you." His compliment warmed her windblown cheeks and she realized that he wasn't seeing things the way she thought.

"I guess I never thought of it before, but how many dogs do you have?"

His question pricked the reservoir behind her eyes and before she could stop it, a tear had leaked out. "I just finished training a Boxer named Charlie. He's with an Army vet."

"Really? When you said you wanted to start a business with service dogs, you didn't mention that you were already training them." Jordan looked at her with admiration. "How long had you been training him?"

"Almost a year." It had been the best thing to train Charlie, but it was so hard to give him away. He was only the third service dog she'd trained, but passing them on hadn't gotten any easier yet.

Jordan wiped away her tear with his thumb. "I'm sorry." He pulled her in close to his chest and the action undid all the brace work she'd built around her heart.

"I can't help falling in love with them even though it wouldn't be right to keep them."

"You're pretty great, you know." Jordan leaned back and smiled at Madison.

She took a shaky breath and smiled back. "So are you."

He cocked his head to the side. "You sure about that?"

"Almost," Madison whispered and she came up on her tiptoes and kissed his cheek. Jordan put his arms around her and turned his head, covering her mouth in a kiss that found the spark from earlier and exploded like a sunburst from her middle. His hands moved down her back and he pulled her closer, breathing in her breaths, kissing her upper lip softly and drawing out each touch of their lips.

She held tight to him, returning each kiss and wanting more. His mouth moved against hers and he drew her impossibly closer while at the same time, she felt like they weren't close enough. When she broke the kiss, Jordan's breath was hot against her cheek and before she could catch her breath, he dipped his head and kissed her jawline and the curve of her neck. He could probably read her pulse through his lips because her blood was singing as her heart pumped wildly for the next kiss.

Madison reached up and put her arms around his neck, kissing his mouth again. Jordan pulled back slightly and said in a husky voice, "I guess I'd better go now."

"But you asked if I was sure," Madison said, her voice dropping a notch. She pulled him closer and kissed him once, twice, three more times and then leaned back. "Yep, you're pretty great."

He chuckled and kissed her once more before releasing her with a groan. "I think this is why I don't leave the office on Saturdays."

"No way." Madison shook a finger at him. "Don't blame me, but do save next Saturday for me, okay?"

Jordan gave her a smoldering look. "If I have to hire ten more people, I will, 'cause next Saturday it's me and you." He held on to her hand as he took a step back. "Good night, Madison."

She locked the door after he left, walked into her tiny living room, and curled up on the couch. Jordan had said he needed her earlier tonight and Madison couldn't deny that she felt the same way. Jordan had only said a few words, but in those words he showed Madison that he truly understood the work she did and how her heart stayed tethered to the dogs she worked with.

And those kisses. Madison's stomach flipped every time she replayed Jordan's kisses in her mind. He'd given her a taste of something that she couldn't do without, so when her inner critic started flinging questions her way about getting involved with a workaholic, Madison shut her off and went to bed. When she closed her eyes she could still feel Jordan's lips on hers. Saturday was much too far away.

Chapter 16

*J*ordan called Madison on his way to work every day the next week. He'd never had a relationship where it was so easy to talk to a woman—and he talked to Madison about all kinds of things. He craved her voice and even more, he craved her kisses. On Monday, he'd met with Porter and told him that things had to change because he wanted to give Madison a fair chance. So every day at ten after two, Porter connected Jordan's office phone to Madison so they could talk because Madison was either on her way into the shelter or on her way home from a shift.

With help from his assistants, Jordan booked a table at the Signature room at the 95th. It was tricky with only ten days lead time for the reservations, but Porter seemed to enjoy making the impossible happen. The top of the John Hancock building was a popular dining spot for the upper class, and he wanted next Saturday to be special. He had tried to rearrange his schedule to at least meet Madison for lunch, but the Falzon account in the city of Shenzhen in China had several issues that needed to be resolved. Jordan ended up doing several video conference calls late in the evening with Porter to sort everything out. He remembered how Lexi had advised him to sell the Falzon account at the same time that he'd sold some other factories in China, but Jordan had resisted. But six months later, he wished he'd taken his sister's advice.

After the third late night in a row dealing with stresses thousands of miles away, Jordan met with Porter and Eric. "I don't want to deal with this account anymore. I want it off my plate by next week and out of Burke Enterprises within the month."

Porter and Eric had looked at each other with raised eyebrows. "You got it, sir. What about the potential investors?"

"Sell it to them if they're interested, but this amount of stress isn't worth the money." When Jordan said the words, he heard the truth of them reverberate through the room. His body shifted and he found that he actually believed it—believed that he could change.

On Thursday, he left work at four o'clock to meet Madison for another training session with Roxie. She was at the house in the back yard with Roxie when he arrived twenty minutes late. Her dark hair was pulled back in a messy bun and she wore a loose fitting off the shoulder tee with a black tank top underneath. Her bronze shoulder in the late afternoon sunlight looked kissable. Jordan reminded himself that today wasn't a date, but he still planned on kissing the beautiful woman in front of him.

"I'm sorry to keep you waiting," Jordan said. "Traffic was a mess today."

"That's okay," she replied. "Roxie and I have been working on a few things."

"You look great." He walked up to her and brushed a kiss over her lips.

Madison smiled and her dark eyes brightened. She put a hand on his cheek. "Everything still a go for this weekend?"

"You bet. I'm working on a pretty big surprise. I hope I can pull it off." He pulled her in for a hug.

"I like the sounds of that, but I'm happy just spending time with you, Jordan."

Jordan felt the impact of her words solidify his decision to offload the Falzon account. For the first time in years, he could imagine a different future for himself. He leaned in and kissed Madison again. "I know when we talked a couple days ago I said I'd have to rush back to the office, but could you stay for dinner?"

"Really?" Madison put her hand out to keep Roxie from jumping while directing her smile at Jordan.

"Yes. I'll have to manage a couple calls, but we'll still have some time. Would that be okay?"

"Sure," Madison replied. She tossed Roxie's ball to her. "I've been looking forward to tasting something made by your personal chef."

Jordan grinned. "Good. Tonight is fish night."

"Then I'm staying for sure. Come on, Roxie. Let's show Jordan how smart you are."

They worked together with Roxie and the puppy showed off how well she could sit, shake, and lie down. Jordan admired how much better Roxie looked in the past month. Her sleek black fur had taken on a healthy shine to it and he could no longer see her ribs. Jordan got down on the ground with Roxie and the little pup immediately climbed onto his lap.

"She always wants to be right next to me or on me," Jordan said.

"That's pretty typical. It might be a lot to think about right now, but you might consider getting another dog as a companion in the future. Maybe one that is a few years older than Roxie."

Jordan's eyes widened. "You're kidding, right? Haven't I told you what Roxie did to my house?"

Madison laughed. "That's why you get a more mellow dog who is three or four years old. One who is already house-trained."

"If I didn't know you better, I'd think you were trying to make me go crazy."

"Oh, don't worry. I already know you're a little bit crazy." Madison stood and patted Roxie's head. "Who else rescues stray dogs from downtown Chicago?"

"Technically she rescued me," Jordan replied. He had told Madison the story of the muggers in the alley and it still amazed him how the little puppy had saved him. He brushed off his pants and took Madison's hand. "Are we done for today?"

"Yes, but I want a closer look at your wishing well." Madison pointed to the wishing well that stood at the edge of his yard.

"Come and see." He tugged on her hand and showed her how the stream of water from the fountain in his yard ran underneath the wishing well so it appeared to be a real well.

"It adds such character to your yard. I love it." Madison leaned over the well and looked inside. She tossed in a penny and then closed her eyes. Her lips moved as she whispered a wish.

Jordan watched her, feeling young again when he and Lexi would play around his parent's old wishing well. Everything about her brought light to his life. "I hope your wish comes true."

Madison looked up and stepped away from the well. "Me too." She looked back at the well, her fingers absently trailing through the loose strands of her hair.

"That must be some wish," Jordan said. "Maybe I better try it."

Madison turned back to him. "Yes, I think you should. What would you wish for, Jordan? If you could have anything in the world, what would it be?"

The answer was on his tongue before he could open his mouth. Jordan tried to swallow it back down, but the way Madison watched him, as if begging him to let her in his heart, made the words heavy on his lips. He leaned forward and looked inside the well, letting his eyes adjust to the darkness, smelling the pungent scent of moss and stone. "I wish I could talk to my dad one more time."

For the past five years, Jordan had tried not to think of that night, but it always hung on the periphery of his memory, staining his grief with a pain that no one could understand. Lexi thought she understood how deeply Jordan felt the loss because she felt the same, but no one understood the added agony that Jordan felt. No one understood that he blamed himself for his parents' death.

"It was my fault." There. He'd finally said it. He stepped away from the wishing well and shoved his hands in his pockets, leaning against the wooden frame attached to the stone well.

Madison's eyes widened. "What do you mean?"

"It's my fault my parents are dead." Jordan's voice sounded flat and hollow to his ears.

"I thought you said they died in a car accident," Madison replied. She put her hand on his arm and the other on his chest. "Tell me what's in here."

If he closed his eyes, he could still hear his father in his authoritative tone telling Jordan to consider veterinary school again. The echoes of the last conversation he'd had with his dad resurfaced. He started talking to Madison as he relived that night.

Jordan clenched the phone tightly and gritted his teeth as he listened to his dad reiterate for the millionth time how important it was to finish his education and stay the course. He was sick of listening to his father's ideas and feeling judged because he wasn't doing everything right.

"Son, I just want what's best for you," his dad said. "I want you to keep your priorities straight."

"Dad, I don't want to go to college. That's your dream. I'll do just fine with this new company and I'm working another job until things take off. I'm being responsible."

"You're being short-sighted. This job may seem like enough for you now, but I've seen it in your eyes—I'm not sure you're really happy."

"Dad, stop."

But his dad didn't stop. He pressed forward. "The Jordan Burke I know loves a challenge and always rises to it. Maybe you won't go to college, but don't do something you don't love just because it makes a lot of money."

"Dad, I don't need your advice or your pep talks. Just let me live my life. There wasn't anybody butting into your life, telling you what to do when you were my age and you turned out fine."

Two breaths of silence pulsed across the phone lines, and he thought he heard his father swallow hard. "You're exactly right, Son. There wasn't anybody to help me, to guide me, to encourage me. Sometimes I wonder how my life might have been different if there had been someone."

"You have different dreams and expectations for me. You always have!" Jordan argued.

The conversation continued to deteriorate—Jordan's voice sharp and cruel in his father's ears. He hung up the phone mid-sentence, angry and frustrated.

Two hours later, the phone rang, but it wasn't his father.

A police officer. There had been a terrible accident involving both his mother and father. He knew the answer but he asked the question anyway, *Where did it happen?*

The police officer affirmed Jordan's fears and he hung up the phone feeling the crushing weight of guilt, knowing that if he hadn't yelled at his father, if instead he'd been a grateful son, his parents might still be alive today.

113

Jordan went quiet, fully feeling the pain from that night. After a while he opened his eyes, the memories burning away in the sunlight that framed Madison's face. "If I close my eyes, I can still hear my dad's voice," he murmured. He'd never told anyone about that night before.

"Oh, Jordan. I'm so sorry." Madison touched his cheek, her eyes brimming with tears. "It wasn't your fault. What you think happened, that car accident wasn't your fault. You weren't even there."

Jordan held her gaze for a moment and he looked away. "No one knows. But I know. Whenever he was upset he would head to the lake. I don't know why Mom was with him, unless she was trying to calm him down. My dog, Ralph, was with them too. He died in the accident along with my parents."

Madison covered her mouth, tears spilling onto her cheeks. "I'm so sorry. You lost everyone."

"I pushed them away. It could have been different. They would still be alive today."

She shook her head and then reached for Jordan's hand. "That doesn't make you responsible. Jordan, why are you carrying this? It's not your fault."

Jordan pushed his hands through his hair and groaned. "Because my dad was right. About everything. If I would've listened to him and given him the respect he deserved from his only son he wouldn't have felt the need to go for a drive to get away from it all. He might have still been on the phone talking to me."

Madison followed him out onto the grass. She tilted her head and rested her hand on his arm. "Even if what you did influenced your dad's actions, you are not responsible for your parents' death. Holding onto this is wrong."

"You don't understand. Think about it. Think about how you would feel if it was your sister."

Madison sucked in a breath. She swallowed and leaned forward. Jordan watched the emotions play out across her face. The pain, sadness, and anguish. Maybe she could understand.

"Okay I thought about it," she said. "It still wouldn't be my fault. We all have a choice and I know your mom and dad would not want you carrying this guilt over their death. I can't think of anything that would make them feel worse than to know that their death caused you so much pain. Jordan, you have to forgive yourself and let this go."

"I don't know how. I've never told anyone before. Not even Lexi."

Madison squeezed his arm. "Well, maybe you should start there. Talk to your sister. I'm sure she will understand and maybe she could shed light on what happened to give you a different perspective. You should call her."

Madison hugged Jordan and when he wrapped his arms around her, he felt different. Something had worked its way free.

She put her hand on his cheek. "It might take some time, but if you'll let yourself, I'm confident that you'll find peace concerning your parents' death."

"Madison, thank you for listening."

"Thank you for telling me. I want to know your heart. You have a good heart." Madison put her small hands on Jordan's chest. He looked down at her hand and covered it with his own.

"I want to know your heart too. If you'll let me."

Madison gave him a half-smile. There was something behind her smile that he didn't know because she hadn't shared it with him yet.

She leaned onto her toes and kissed him and his worries faded away to nothing as he held her in his arms.

Chapter 17

Kissing Jordan was better than eating, but Madison's stomach growled anyway. Jordan chuckled and pulled away. "We'd better head into the dining room."

Madison put a hand over her stomach and frowned. "I guess."

Jordan leaned in and gave her another quick kiss. "Save some room for dessert." He waggled his eyebrows and Madison felt the back of her neck turn warm. She didn't know how to explain it, but every minute she spent with Jordan, he was more attractive. She had memorized the way he tilted his head to one side when he was thinking hard about something, and she loved the little quirk of his mouth when he was thinking about kissing her. He was kind, all man, and now that he had opened up and told her about the guilt he carried, she finally understood why he looked so vulnerable at the same time his muscles were rippling under his shirt.

When Madison had first visited Jordan's home, she never would have anticipated that she would be sitting next to him at his extravagant dining room table, holding his hand, or kissing his gorgeous mouth. But as his staff brought in the meal prepared by his personal chef and a warm plate with steaming halibut was put in front of her, Madison sat back and enjoyed every moment. If it was a dream, she hoped she wouldn't wake up. The naysayer in her head that whispered for her to focus on how tenuous their relationship was because it would always come in second to Jordan's company was pushed to the side. Madison took a bite of the tender halibut and stared at the man she was falling in love with. Yes, Jordan had been a workaholic, but he was changing and Madison was willing to give him a chance.

"Thanks for staying for dinner," Jordan said. He glanced at his watch. "In twelve minutes I have to head to my office for that conference call, but I hope you'll stay."

"I have some appointments I need to set up with two new clients next week, so I'll try to reach them then."

Jordan reached over and squeezed her hand. "Thanks, Maddie. You would be so proud of me if you could see the changes that are happening."

"Like what?"

"Well, for starters, I'm here, eating dinner in my own house at a normal hour instead of talking to China until eleven at night."

Madison shuddered. "I am proud of you. I can't wait to see what things look like when you only work forty hours a week."

Jordan cringed. "Yeah, me too."

"Hey, don't sound so optimistic," Madison teased. "Stranger things have happened."

He took a bite of fish. "I turned my phone off three times."

Madison gave a mock gasp of surprise. "The world may be ending. Should we go down to the bunker? You have a bunker right?"

"You're funny. I might have to keep you around just for the laughs."

Madison rolled her eyes and puckered her lips. "I'm sure that's the only reason you'd keep me around."

Jordan's cheeks reddened and Madison laughed, surprised that she'd been able to throw him off ground. They continued to banter through the meal until an alarm sounded on Jordan's phone. He frowned. "I feel bad about this. Are you sure you're okay?"

Madison nodded. "I'm sure as long as you come back to me."

Jordan stood and grabbed his phone. He hesitated, and then turned back to her, rounded the table and kissed her full on the mouth. "I'll definitely be back."

She watched him stride from the room, and then she fanned her face with her napkin. She pulled out her phone and texted Sue: **I think I might be falling in love.**

Thirty seconds later her phone dinged with a reply: **You go girl!**

Madison smiled. Sue was rooting for her, and her wise friend's support solidified Madison's decision to go all in with Jordan.

About forty minutes later, Madison had contacted all of her clients and updated her calendar for the next three weeks. She leaned her head back against the couch and looked at the clock. It was nearly eight o'clock and Jordan said he usually wasn't even home from the office at this time. She wondered if he'd thought much about his future with any kind of family in it. Madison longed for the picture book family—the one she'd missed out on. She dreamed about a father who adored his wife and children, who hurried home from work to spend time with the family and saved up his vacation days to go camping with everyone, including the family dogs. It was probably unrealistic and maybe even unlikely, but it was her dream and she wasn't ready to give up on it yet.

Her father had willingly given that dream away—thrown it away, actually. When Abigail's epileptic attacks increased, and her general health declined, instead of holding tighter to his family, he had left. For years he had told Madison that he made the choice to provide for their family by working extra to pay medical bills. Madison had believed him until she grew old enough to understand how the world worked and that her father wasn't working twenty-four hours a day. He could have come home if he wanted to, but he didn't want to be there. Her father chose his job over his family and that memory frightened Madison even as Jordan's kisses lingered on her lips.

She closed her eyes and drew in a deep breath. Just because Jordan had been a workaholic for most of his adult life did not mean that he would abandon his family. Madison chose to focus on the evidence she'd seen in Jordan—the little changes he was making to try to spend more time with her. She didn't like feeling afraid that every successful businessman was like her father—putting his job before his family. Madison opened her eyes, taking in her surroundings and noting the feeling of Jordan's home. He had a long way to go in balancing his work and life, but she believed that his intentions were good.

"Hey, beautiful. Sorry that took me a little longer than I hoped." Jordan interrupted her thoughts as he walked around the couch. He sat next to Madison, draping his arm across the back of the couch. His top two buttons were undone and it looked like he'd run his hands through his hair. She reached up and trailed her fingers over the unruly hair by his ears.

"It turned out okay. I got some work done too."

Jordan propped his bare feet up on the coffee table in front of them. Madison had never seen him quite so relaxed. She cozied up next to him and he smiled. "Did I mention that you're so pretty you drive me crazy?"

Madison trailed her fingers along the bit of scruff on his jawline. "Hmm, maybe not those exact words, but you could tell me again if you want."

"Come here, beautiful." He pulled her onto his lap and kissed her. His lips were soft, yet hungry for her and she tasted the mint in his mouth as he deepened the kiss. Madison sighed, leaning her head back as he planted tender kisses along her neck. She put her arms around him, her fingers digging into his thick hair. They kissed, letting everything else fade into the background. In that moment, Madison forgot every doubt she'd had about him. His hands on her felt right, his kisses claimed her as his, and she wanted to be his.

Jordan leaned his head back and cleared his throat. "Wow, I think we might have skipped dessert."

Madison giggled and kissed him again. "Maybe we'd better go see what they have prepared."

"I know we should, but I don't want to let you go."

"Then don't." Madison laid her head against his chest and he brushed his fingers over her hair.

He rubbed her back in a slow circle. "You think we could do this?"

His voice was husky and for a second, Madison wasn't sure if she'd heard him right. She lifted her head and when their eyes met heat flared in her chest. "I'd like to try," she whispered.

Jordan smiled and he held her close and kissed the top of her forehead. "I need you, Madison."

She could feel his heart beating against her cheek and she felt a need for him that she hadn't realized before. She wanted to stay right there in his arms, safe, and loved. "Jordan," she murmured, but he kissed away the words before she could say them.

Chapter 18

The following Monday Jordan had roses delivered to the animal shelter for Madison. He also sent a bag of dog biscuits and an assortment of chew toys for her furry friends. He'd hinted that there was something special planned for this weekend, but he hadn't told her what yet. Everyone was working overtime to pull together the details for the sale of the Falzon account. Several investors would be flying into Chicago this weekend. In the past, he would go out to dinner with the investors and they would talk business before signing the deal.

The upscale restaurant for this venue would be The Signature Room at the 95th and Jordan planned to bring Madison along to the final signing so that she could see exactly how much he had changed to bring her into his life. He wanted her to understand the significance of this shift in his company and how it would affect their future together. To help her see what she meant to him.

He couldn't get enough of Madison. They'd been together in between every conference call and meeting over the weekend and letting her go home the night before had been more difficult than the last company merger he'd overseen. Everywhere he turned he saw something that made him think of Madison. He was a desert and she was his oasis.

"Sir? You missed your 11:15 call," Porter's voice came over his speaker phone. "Would you like me to put them through now?"

Jordan rubbed a hand over his face. "Yes, sorry. Hey, Porter, how are the plans coming for this Saturday?"

"Good, sir. The people from the Falzon account will be here Friday to go over everything, so you should be good to go."

"Thank you. Any chance you could find me some time Thursday to spend with Madison?"

"Like I said the last time you asked, uh, two hours ago, I haven't been able to create any openings but I'm trying my best."

Jordan groaned, and he heard Porter laugh. "Just say it," he grumbled.

"I think it would be a nice touch to get her a piece of jewelry."

"She's not really the jewelry type. She works with dogs all day."

"What about a watch?"

"That might work. Could you look into that a little more for me? I think she'd like something that she could just slip on her wrist."

"I'm on it."

"And Porter?"

"Yes, sir?"

"You didn't say it, so I will. I've got it bad for this girl and I'm willing to do whatever it takes to spend time with her. I need you to help me fix my life so that I can have a family. It's past time."

There was a pause and Porter cleared his throat. "That sounds like a good plan. I'll get to work on it."

"Thank you."

Over the next two days, Jordan continued to spend every spare moment on the details for closing out the Falzon account. On Friday, he called Madison.

"Hey, gorgeous."

"Hey, yourself. I miss you."

His senses perked up at the sound of her voice. "I've been working double-time this week so that I don't have to again. Things are really coming together, Maddie. I'm going to be able to have a normal life."

"I love it when you talk sweet to me."

"Well, tomorrow I'm going to do more than talk to you."

Madison giggled. "Jordan!"

"What? I meant I'm going to treat you to a fancy dinner at the Signature Room. Wear your best dress. I have something special for you."

"Okay."

He heard hesitation in her voice. "You don't have to wear a dress, Maddie. Business pants will do just fine."

"Okay, I'll be ready." There was still hesitation in her voice, and maybe a note of worry.

After they said goodbye, Jordan thought of two things. Number one: He hadn't told Madison he loved her yet and he was ready to say the "L" word, but he didn't want it to be over the phone. Number two: He needed Lexi's help to find a dress for Madison.

He picked up his cell and called his sister.

"Jordy! You're calling me. Is everything okay?"

Jordan chuckled. "It's better than okay, Lexi. I'm in love." He held the phone away, but Lexi's squeal was still ear-splitting.

"Tell me everything," she demanded.

"Okay, but I only have eight minutes so it'll have to be the abbreviated version."

"I'm listening."

Nine minutes later, Jordan had shared the details of how Madison had single-handedly stolen his heart. He'd explained his plan to off-load the Falzon account and free up time in his life for a relationship. That led to the situation of the date at the Signature Room and the dilemma of finding a dress when he didn't know what size Madison wore. Lexi asked for Madison's number, reassuring him that she'd take care of everything.

"Don't mess this up, Jordy. I've never heard you like this before and I can't wait to see Madison's face next to yours this January."

Jordan couldn't tame his smile once he'd ended the call, so he ended up in his next meeting with a goofy grin and he didn't even try to explain it away.

Madison's feet ached by the time she finished her shift on Friday and she was so grateful for the chance to sit down that she almost missed the note on her door about a delivery downstairs. With a groan, she went downstairs to the apartment office to figure out what had come in the mail that wouldn't fit in her slot.

"You must be doing something fun this weekend," Linda said as she lifted two dress bags from a pile of boxes behind her.

"Wait, where did these come from?"

"Special delivery from Jordan Burke is what the ticket says. Do you know him?"

Madison grinned. "Yes, I do know him. Thanks, Linda."

She took the dress bags upstairs to her apartment and unzipped them as soon as the door closed behind her. She gasped when the light hit the rhinestones sewn onto the dark green cocktail dress. The fabric was lightweight and silky soft and when Madison held it up, she imagined Jordan's face when he saw her. She had to give it to him. Even though he was a workaholic, he could definitely work some magic. How had he known that she didn't own a fancy dress?

The second dress was stunning. It was floor-length with a slit up the thigh. The fabric was a deep orange that would look great against her dark hair and bronzed skin. When she went to zip up the bags she found designer shoes in her size that matched each dress perfectly. Madison almost pinched herself because it seemed impossible that she had found someone as perfect as Jordan. He hadn't said the words yet, but she could sense his love in everything he did.

Jordan kept saying that he had something special planned for their date on Saturday—a surprise. Madison's heart pounded as she considered what the surprise might be. For a billionaire, the options were unlimited, but she had a feeling that whatever Jordan had planned, it was not something that would flaunt his wealth. That wasn't his way.

Madison grabbed her phone and called him, excited to thank him for the dresses. His phone went directly to voice mail so she settled on leaving a message and then texted him too. He had said he was working hard so that he wouldn't be so busy anymore. She didn't understand exactly what that meant or how he would accomplish it, but as she tried on the green dress, she figured if he could find two perfect cocktail dresses then he could figure out how to fix his work schedule to be with the woman he loved. Hopefully.

Chapter 19

The Falzon account hit a few snags on Friday, and everything wasn't going exactly how Jordan had planned. There were a few technicalities with the sale and the prospective buyers insisted on meeting with their investors before making the sale final. The only thing that kept Jordan from pulling his hair out was thinking of how that would ruin his chances for Madison to run her fingers through it.

He went into work early on Saturday and put everything in place to close out the sale that night. It might be a long shot, but he still wanted to show Madison physical proof that he wasn't letting his business run him anymore. Jordan showered and changed at his office and promised himself that he would figure out a way to break that habit. The spacious shower in his master suite was woefully underused.

Madison had called and left a message last night, excited about the dresses but Jordan had received the message too late to call her back. He settled for a text and then sent thanks to Lexi as well. He wanted this night to be perfect, but he was so tense that he felt like he was sitting too close to an electric fence. Exhaustion crept in from every corner of his body, but Jordan pushed through because tonight he was going to tell Madison he loved her. Then he would show her his new schedule—the one with family time highlighted each night, except for the weeks he had to be in China. A part of him knew that he was still working too many hours each week and a trip to China every two months for ten days made the family time a lot smaller than he wanted, but at least he was starting somewhere.

At five o'clock, Jordan exited the quiet building and got into the limo waiting for him. They drove to pick up Madison and Jordan worked on a few more emails during the drive. By the time he finished checking everything with his assistants, Jordan felt a renewed sense of anticipation. It was really happening. He would surprise Madison tonight and tell her that he loved her.

When they pulled up to her apartment, he turned his phone on silent and slid it into the pocket of his suit jacket. Tonight was for Madison. The cellophane crinkled when he picked up the two dozen sterling roses he'd special ordered from a hothouse in Virginia. Their aroma was subtle, yet stunning, just like the light lavender color of the petals. He jogged up the flight of stairs to her apartment, his breath coming fast more from excitement than the exertion. He knocked lightly on the door and held the roses out in front of him so when Madison opened the door he could just see her face over the top of the roses.

"Jordan, these are beautiful! Thank you." She took the roses and hugged him.

She wore the green cocktail dress that had been his favorite when Lexi sent the pictures. It came just above her knee and wrapped snug across her tiny waist. The v-neck revealed just enough to make Jordan wish that Madison was already his wife. "You are absolutely gorgeous and I am in trouble," Jordan murmured as he leaned forward to kiss Madison. She pressed her open lips to his and Jordan pulled her closer, the cellophane on the roses crinkling.

Madison put a hand on his chest and pulled away. "It's a good thing I didn't have my lipstick on yet." She winked and he followed her through the door of her apartment, mesmerized by her beauty.

She walked into her small kitchen and reached up above the sink for a vase for the roses. Her shapely calves flexed as she moved and Jordan noticed the shiny silver heels she wore. "I'm glad you liked the dress. My sister Lexi is pretty amazing because that dress looks like it was made for you."

"Thank you." Her eyes flicked to his and he wondered if she could see the hungry desire in his gaze. He took a deep breath and blew it out slowly as Madison arranged the flowers. The bouquet dominated the room and the light aroma filled the air.

She walked around the edge of the counter and stood in front of Jordan. "I've been looking forward to this night all week. Thank you for making me feel like a princess tonight. Just give me a minute to put on my lipstick."

"Wait," he grabbed her hand and pulled it up to his chest. She could probably feel his heart beating where her hand rested, but he didn't care. He pulled her to him and covered her mouth in a kiss that heated his belly and made him forget anything about dinner. The skin of her neck was smooth and soft and he covered it with kisses, trailing down along the silky neckline of her dress. Madison put a hand on his cheek and said in a husky voice, "I think I'd better go put on my lipstick now."

"Madison, I—I need you."

She smiled. "I'll be right back."

Jordan watched her walk back to her bedroom. He'd almost told her he loved her, but he'd chickened out at the last second. Now he wished he could go back and say it boldly so she wouldn't have any doubt in her mind what he meant when he said, I need you.

Jordan led Madison out of the building to where a sleek limo awaited them. "A limo! Thanks, Jordan. I really do feel like a princess."

"You are my princess." He helped her inside the limo and put his arm around her. Back in her apartment when he'd told her that he needed her, Madison thought for a second that he was going to say he loved her. She felt it in every kiss and the tender way he held her in his arms. Madison held his hand and felt like the luckiest woman in the world as the limo driver maneuvered through the downtown Chicago traffic. She wanted to tell her mom about Jordan but she needed to be sure about him first. Her mother would tell her only surviving daughter to run as far as she could from a busy executive like Jordan. But Jordan had constantly surprised her over the past few weeks. He really was making an effort to change his priorities to include a relationship.

Jordan tucked a strand of hair behind her ear. "Hey gorgeous, what's on your beautiful mind?"

Madison smiled. "I was just thinking that if it weren't for Roxie, I never would have met you."

He chuckled. "She sure is a lot of trouble, but it's been worth it." He ran his thumb over her knuckles. "Thanks for being so patient with me. I'm really excited about some things I have in the works."

"Like what?"

"Oh, no. I'm not talking about work tonight. I only want to talk about you...and me. Us." He kissed her cheek softly.

Madison met his gaze and her stomach tumbled with emotion. There was so much that she didn't know about Jordan yet—so much that he didn't know about her. It was scary, but she wanted to take the risk. She felt like she was standing on the edge of a cliff and Jordan was her parachute. She took a shaky breath.

"Us?" She brushed a feather-light kiss across his lips. "I like the sound of that."

Jordan cleared his throat. "Have you thought any more about the training center you want to set up?"

Madison loved the way that Jordan tried so hard to be a gentleman when it was obvious he'd like nothing more than to kiss her senseless. She leaned into him. "I'm thinking about cutting some of my hours at the shelter so that I'll have more time to devote to training a new service dog."

"That sounds like a start, but it's really just you and one dog. It sounded to me like you wanted the opportunity to work with several trainers, right?"

He remembered the details of her business idea. Madison fell a little more in love with him. "That is what I want, but if I start putting the word out that I'm training others, I need to be ready. I haven't been able to find a good location that would work year-round."

Jordan rubbed the scruff along his chin. "Isn't it interesting how location can often be the toughest part about setting up a new business?"

"Yes, everything is so expensive or if it's a reasonable price, it can't accommodate that many dogs. I might have to do more one-on-one training to help others get certified to train, but I still want to be involved in the entire process so that the dogs coming from my program would be vetted by me."

"How can I help you, Maddie?" Jordan's face was eager and his eyes sparkled with enthusiasm. "Will you let me help you with your dream?"

Madison looked down at their hands clasped together. It would be so easy for Jordan. He'd make a few phone calls, drop money wherever needed, and the business would be a reality, but she didn't want him to feel obligated to her. The funding would make everything else easier, but what about their future? She couldn't risk her entire business on the what-if of her relationship with a billionaire.

"I don't know how to explain it, but I feel like I need to do this, to build it on my own." She lifted her eyes to his, worried that he would be hurt by her answer.

"I get it." He nodded. "There must be something I can do, though. Please?"

Madison smiled when his voice pitched upwards in a plea. "Well, I wouldn't turn away good help. Let me think things through first. When I get to a point where I'm ready, I'll ask you first."

"Promise?"

She hesitated. That word meant so much to her. It reminded her of wedding vows, of broken promises that her father scattered like ashes on her family. And then there was a promise of a new future from her mom—that everything would be fine, but it wasn't because Abigail had died and her mom had shriveled to a shell of her former self. She'd taught Madison to be distrusting of men and so she'd pushed away several guys who didn't have clear priorities for their lives. In hindsight, she had perhaps been harsher than was reasonable because of her fears. If Jordan was changing, so could she.

"I promise." Madison squeezed his hand and looked out the window at the busy streets around them. She would let her heart be free and open tonight because she was in love with Jordan Burke.

 **Chapter 20**

The restaurant was absolutely spectacular with an incredible view of Chicago's varied skyscrapers and historic buildings. Jordan eagerly pulled Madison toward the window beyond their table and pointed out the Sears Tower, the Chicago Plaza, and the AT&T towers. Madison had grown up in Chicago, but she'd never seen a view like this before.

"I heard the best view is from the women's restroom, but I've never seen it myself," Jordan said.

Madison laughed. "Well, I guess I'll have to check that out later and I'll let you know."

Jordan seemed a bit nervous as the hostess led them through the restaurant to a large room. They had just entered the room when a burly man clapped Jordan on the shoulder.

"Jordan, I'm impressed with how you've handled the business of this sale."

Jordan glanced at Madison, and shook the man's hand. "Thank you. How are you, Mr. Linton?"

"Fine, fine. I have to say that I'm really glad to see you here. I've been at odds with my investors over how to get this sale finalized and I really needed you to explain to them one more time what you explained to me."

Madison saw a flash of panic cross Jordan's face and he clenched one hand in a fist and then stretched his fingers out slowly. "Mr. Linton, that's why we're here. I'd be happy to go over any questions they might have."

The man shook his head. "I hope we can get this figured out. The Patton investors are only here for today and then they are flying back to New York. One of your associates has already been talking with them, but I have to say that I can tell they aren't impressed." Mr. Linton put a hand to the side of his mouth and lowered his voice. "If we can't get them on board, then I may have to back out of this sale."

Real panic showed in Jordan's eyes. He straightened, and lifted Madison's hand, encouraging her to stand next to him. "This is Madison Poplawski. I've asked her to dine with me this evening. Madison, this is Mr. Alfred Linton. I've worked with him for many years and his company is looking at taking on some business from Burke Enterprises."

Madison tried to read Jordan's expression. He didn't seem particularly surprised to see a business associate at the restaurant and Mr. Linton acted as if he expected Jordan to conduct business during the meal. This couldn't be part of the surprise Jordan had planned, so what was going on? Madison pasted on a smile and reached out her hand. "It's a pleasure to meet you."

He pressed the edge of her fingers in a soft hand shake. "The pleasure is mine. She is a sight, Jordan. Where did you find her?"

"She's actually my personal dog trainer. It's been an eventful few weeks."

Mr. Linton nodded and his eyes flicked up and down Madison's dress. "I guess money really can buy happiness. Well, come on then. Let's not keep the Pattons waiting any longer."

Before Jordan could say a word, Mr. Linton was marching across the room and Jordan looked after him. He tugged Madison's hand. "I can't believe my luck," he grumbled. "Maddie, I'm so sorry. I had this all planned out. I wanted it to be a surprise—it still can be if you can trust me. Do you understand?"

Madison furrowed her brow. Jordan hadn't had the chance to correct Mr. Linton and let him know that she was his dog trainer and his girlfriend. It bothered her, but Jordan was by her side now. She straightened and looked up at him. "I'm not sure, but I trust you Jordan."

Jordan blew out a breath and pressed his lips together. "It's still going to work out, but if I don't go talk with that man, I can kiss any chance of a real life goodbye."

Madison followed after him, confused by what was happening. There had been a sale mentioned, but was it really worth so much money that Jordan thought his way of life was at stake?

As they walked across the room, Madison noted that there were less than ten people there. Mr. Linton was heading for a couple near the bar and Madison blanched when he reached the couple and turned to motion for Jordan.

The woman wore a sparkly gold gown with a split more than halfway up her thigh. There was a matching slit in the bodice that almost went down to her belly button and there definitely wasn't enough fabric on the dress to cover her surgically altered chest. She had six inch high gold heels and she towered over her pudgy husband. As they approached, Madison decided that maybe the man was her father, because she looked closer to Madison's age.

"Jordan, this is Carlotta Patton and her husband, Sergio." Mr. Linton introduced them and Madison bit back her surprise. *They were married?*

Carlotta teetered forward on her high heels, and she ignored Jordan's outstretched hand. She crushed her voluptuous bosom against him and kissed each of his cheeks. "Oh, Sergio, isn't he a delight?"

Sergio raised his glass and then drained it in one gulp. Mr. Linton looked over at Madison and inclined his head. "This is Jordan's personal dog trainer. She'll be dining with us tonight as well."

Madison felt like she'd been slapped when Mr. Linton introduced her again as Jordan's dog trainer. The blood rushed to her cheeks and she opened her mouth to correct him this time, to let him know that she was Jordan's girlfriend, but stopped when she saw Carlotta turn toward her with narrowed eyes. "Charmed."

She turned back to Jordan and linked arms with him. "Now, you must explain to me again about this Falzon account because Sergio is out of sorts tonight and he wants to head back home. I'd like to sign the papers before we leave, you know." She ran long nails that were painted in a shimmery gold up and down his arm. Carlotta propelled Jordan forward to a server holding a tray of appetizers.

Another server approached Madison and offered her a flute of champagne, but she declined. Her stomach was in knots over these people who had hijacked her date. She swiveled, searching for Jordan and found him across the room. As Madison approached, she watched as Carlotta leaned in, whispering something in Jordan's ear, her lips close enough to leave a tiny smudge of red on his earlobe. She dabbed at her chest with a cloth napkin and then waved it in the air at him. "You're so young. It amazes me that you've been able to build such a business. Sergio has spent his entire life building his empire."

"Yes, he's done very well. I think the Falzon account will thrive within that empire," Jordan replied stiffly. "Will you excuse me for a moment?" Jordan disengaged himself from Carlotta and hurried to Madison.

"Maddie, this isn't what I had planned. I don't know what to do. I've tried reaching my other assistant, Shawn, but he won't be here for another hour. I'm so sorry."

"It's okay. We're still eating together, I guess."

Jordan frowned. "I promise I'll explain later."

Madison nodded as another man came up to Jordan and began asking questions about the mysterious Falzon account. She tried not to think about how this felt familiar—like a page out of her teenage years when her father would schedule time to be with her and end up working the entire time. Madison shook her head. Dwelling on the negatives of her past wouldn't help her tonight.

Maybe it wouldn't hurt to try one of the appetizers rotating around the room, or a glass of bubbly. Madison walked a few paces to a server holding smoked salmon and slices of mango. She was reaching toward a plate when she heard a hiss from behind her.

Carlotta made narrowed her eyes. "So, a dog trainer, huh? I guess they'll let anyone in here as long as they're with Jordan."

"I'm his—"

"Girlfriend?" Carlotta laughed and the sound was harsh and grating on Madison's ears. "In your dreams. Jordan can have anyone he wants and I have a feeling he might want to seal this deal with a kiss if you know what I mean."

The heat of embarrassment touched her cheeks as Carlotta spoke. Madison swallowed back bile in her throat.

"If you care at all about Jordan's company, you won't interfere with any aspect of this deal." She smiled, but it seemed like venom dripped from the side of her lip as she turned and headed back to Jordan.

Madison was speechless. She felt rage enveloping her. She'd never been in a situation like this before—in a room full of people who all seemed threatening in their own way.

Servers in tuxedos started bringing in all kinds of foods. Madison had looked forward to perusing the elegant menu and choosing something superbly crafted just for her, but instead it looked like it would be a buffet. Jordan started heading in her direction only to be grabbed by Carlotta's claws again. He glanced at Madison and then refocused his attention on Carlotta. Hot disappointment sizzled along her nerves. Madison felt alone in this crowd of business associates. *Be reasonable*, Madison repeated to herself. Jordan had said it had something to do with his business. Mr. Linton had explained there was a sale that was supposed to go through. But everything seemed wrong. What had started out as the most romantic night of her life was being hijacked by the woman with golden claws.

Madison walked along the perimeter of the room, trying to focus on the beautiful décor, but her mind was a blur of worry. This night was turning out to be like so many from her past where her father had rejected her for work.

"Darling, have you seen the view from the women's restroom?" Carlotta asked in her purring tone.

Madison jumped at the appearance of the woman, who minutes ago was clinging to Jordan. "I haven't yet," Madison answered in a tight voice.

"Well, what are you waiting for? Go on, you can't miss the best view from The Signature Room."

"Oh, I was really—"

"Really, you must go before they bring out the main dish."

"Okay, that's a good idea." Madison agreed, but only to get the crazy woman out of range. She walked from the room and just before she exited she turned to see if Jordan had even noticed her moving away from him. He was deep in conversation with Mr. Linton and Sergio.

Madison walked down the hallway until she found the women's restroom. Dark cabinetry surrounded the sinks that butted up against the window. Madison sucked in a breath at the gorgeous panoramic view before her. She stepped to the window and gazed out at the city. For a moment, she pretended that her heart wasn't aching and that she really was just visiting the ladies room to powder her nose before returning to her incredibly handsome and thoughtful boyfriend, Jordan Burke.

Her eyes burned and she blinked back tears. Now wasn't the time. She could get through this night. She wasn't a quitter. She stared out at the vista and took a moment to admire the beauty of Chicago's skyline. The setting sun cast a pinkish glow on the lake. City lights were popping up everywhere as darkness fell. The skyscrapers loomed in before her, and Madison took a breath and made a decision. She would go back in the banquet room and if Jordan noticed her, if he gave her even a brief glance, she would stay. It was silly but it was all her heart could handle at the moment so she walked carefully in her high heels, the skirt of her dress swishing around her knees. She entered the banquet room and paused. Her stomach tightened and hunger gnawed on the edges of her sadness. She hadn't been able to eat a bite yet. Carlotta had her arm looped through Jordan's and he stood with his back ramrod straight facing a group of business executives.

Madison took three steps forward, willing Jordan to turn around. But he didn't. She could be the bigger person and walk over to him, stand on the other side of Carlotta the vampire, but why? Madison's shoulders slumped and she turned around. At the door she paused and looked back one more time. This time the only one who noticed her exit was Carlotta. The woman blew her an air kiss and wiggled her fingers as if she'd expected Madison to leave all along. There was a war going on inside Madison's head. One part urging her to stay and fight for the man she loved and the other part mentally shaking her, chanting, *I told you so, told you so.*

As she rode the elevator downstairs she wondered why she ever thought she had a chance with Jordan. What she had just witnessed tonight was probably a regular occurrence for him.

He didn't seem like the type to consort with women like Carlotta but he hadn't done anything to disengage from her viselike grips or to keep Madison by his side.

Jordan had ignored her. He didn't even know that she was gone and Madison felt like a fool for trusting her heart to someone like him—someone like her father. At the street level, Madison caught a taxi and headed home. She breathed in and out slowly, blinking rapidly, holding the tears at bay until she walked through her apartment door.

Chapter 21

The Burke Enterprises' attorney explained the details of where Sergio Patton needed to sign. Jordan felt like his insides were about to explode. He still couldn't believe the irony of his life. To plan a special date for Madison and have it hijacked by the very sale that was supposed to free up more time. They were supposed to eat a leisurely meal and then Jordan would show her the forms, explain what it meant for him and his business and sign them.

He bent over the papers with a pen, surrounded by investors, and eager to get them off his back. The form was notarized after Jordan signed his name. He felt the pressure slide off his back and he straightened, gazing around the room, but Madison was nowhere to be found.

"If you're looking for your little dog trainer, she went to the restroom to check out the view." Carlotta patted his hand.

"We talked about that earlier. I'm glad she has a chance to see it."

"Well, Jordan, we'd better not let all of this good food go to waste." Mr. Linton steered Jordan toward the table with several entrées on warming platters. Jordan ate a few appetizers and was pulled into another conversation with Mr. Linton about a factory in China he had his eye on. When he finished with that conversation, Jordan looked at his watch and realized that over twenty minutes had passed since he'd signed the papers. Carlotta mentioned that Madison was in the restroom, but she hadn't returned. Jordan felt the stuffed mushrooms like rocks in his gut. By trying to make more time for her, he'd ruined everything. He went to the door and looked down the hall hoping to see Madison. Finally he asked a waitress if she would check in the restroom for Madison. The waitress returned, shaking her head. There was no one of Madison's description anywhere in the restaurant.

Jordan panicked. What if something had happened to Madison? But even as he thought about kidnappers or terrorists, Jordan knew that the thing that had happened to Madison was his fault. Worry tightened his lungs and Jordan stepped into the lobby and dialed Madison's number. If she wasn't in the restaurant, then she must have left. She didn't answer the call. He left her a message and then texted an apology asking if he could meet her somewhere.

Finally he returned to the banquet room and told his assistant that he would be leaving. Before he could leave, Carlotta sidled up next to him.

"You're not leaving yet are you?" she crooned.

Jordan cringed inwardly and put on a neutral face. The woman was despicable, but she had urged her husband to purchase his share of the Falzon account. "Yes, I have another important meeting that I need to make it to."

"If you're ever in New York, I hope you'll stop by and say hello."

"I need to go and find my girlfriend," Jordan replied.

Carlotta jutted out her lower lip in a pout. "Your girlfriend? I didn't know you were attached." She put her arm around his waist and pressed her body against his, slithering her other arm up and around his neck. "I'm not busy tonight if you're free," she whispered in his ear. Jordan backed away. "I'm very busy, Carlotta. I hope you'll excuse me." Jordan strode from the banquet room before she could say another word.

Madison changed out of her dress, not even bothering to hang it up as the tears streamed down her face. How long would it take Jordan to figure out that she had left? She wasn't going to wait and see. She changed into jeans and a T-shirt, washed mascara streaks from her face and headed back out the door.

When Jordan finally called and then texted and then called again, Madison was already on her way to the shelter, riding the L. She was grateful she hadn't told her mother about Jordan yet, but she needed help from a friend. Sue was working late that night and she would understand. Madison had experienced heartache, and perhaps in her younger years she might have described an ending to those relationships as heartbreaking, but she realized now that she had never experienced heartbreak like this before. She kept pushing thoughts of Jordan from her mind because it was simply too painful.

When she arrived at the shelter, Madison didn't go inside. She wasn't prepared to tell Sue that the excited hope she'd held for that evening was for naught. She drug her feet, trudging forward, every step taking her farther away from Jordan. She kicked at a rock, and it skittered across the pavement as she walked around the side of the shelter and sat on the hard cement. The side of the building was warm in the darkness and Madison leaned against it with a shuddering cry. She couldn't hold the tears back, even though she'd already cried and washed away the tears at her apartment. Apparently her heart had stored up a vast well of tears that pushed against her chest, rising up her throat, and burning the backs of her eyes.

The sobs shook the air from her lungs and even though her heart must still be beating because she was alive, she couldn't feel it, couldn't hear it. Every breath was painful and Madison couldn't think, couldn't see. She had known that Jordan would hurt her just like her father had, but she'd fooled herself into believing that he would be different.

 **Chapter 22**

The shelter loomed in the darkness as the limo pulled slowly into the parking lot. Jordan scanned the area for any sign of Madison. When he didn't find her at her apartment, he'd headed for the animal shelter because it was the only other place he knew that Madison would have wanted to go, although he doubted she would head there in the fancy green dress. Jordan gritted his teeth, angry at how the night had played out. Yes, he'd succeeded in off-loading the Falzon account, but he'd ruined his chance to tell Madison how he felt about her—how much he loved her.

Jordan stepped out of his car and walked toward the front door. Movement from the side of the building caught his eye and he veered in that direction when he recognized Madison sitting on the cement, her head on her knees.

"Maddie?"

She jerked her head up, her mouth hung open for a second, and hurt flashed through her eyes. "Go away." She lowered her head to her knees again.

Jordan crouched next to her. "Maddie, please let me explain. Everything got out of hand tonight, but I was able to sell off a large company and that will free up more time in the coming weeks."

Madison sniffled and turned her head. Jordan's gut clenched at the tear trailing down her cheek. "I thought you had changed. But you're just the same."

Jordan reached for her but she flinched. "Please, Madison. Don't do this. You don't understand. I can explain."

"You already explained. I'm just your dog trainer and there are more important people waiting for you." There was steel in her voice as she stood up and brushed her hands off. "It's enough. Goodbye." Madison faced forward and walked around the building and in the front door of the shelter.

The earth was solid under Jordan's feet and he concentrated on that. He didn't want to think about his heart. He didn't want to think about the pain, and anguish, or the look on Madison's face just before she walked away. He turned and walked to his car. There had to be some way to fix this, but right then all he could do was breathe in and out.

Jordan rode home in silence, unaware of anything around him. He kept replaying the night in his mind, trying to figure out what he could have done to salvage the situation. The scenario was a dead end no matter how many alternate routes he came up with. Every path led to the same conclusion—the one with Madison walking away, trampling his heart under her feet.

He loved her, but he hadn't told her. Should he have told her tonight at the animal shelter? Jordan pressed his lips firmly together. The way she'd looked at him, nothing he could have said would have made a difference.

Jordan entered through the mud room and groaned when Roxie wasn't there to meet him. He hurried through the house, searching for her, dreading what he might find. He walked past his office and everything stuttered to a stop. His heart stilled, his breath caught, and time blurred.

The office was covered with scraps of paper, chewed up water bottles, shredded napkins, and debris. But those items weren't what had stopped Jordan cold in the doorway of the office. The box of mementos from his parents' home had been pulled out of his office closet. If Jordan hadn't known that Roxie was responsible, he would think the box had exploded.

"Roxie!" Jordan yelled, looking around, but not seeing the black lab. "Roxie, come here!"

He heard her claws skittering along the hardwood floor of the kitchen and she appeared in the doorway, her tail wagging and a happy look in her eyes. Jordan pointed at the mess in his office. "No, no, Roxie! This is such a mess!"

Roxie cowered with her tail between her legs, a soft whine escaping. Jordan sighed, pushing his hands through his hair. The box had sat in his closet untouched for five years now. The anniversary of his parents' death was only a week away and in that moment, with their personal belongings scattered across his floor, the pain felt as sharp as it did the day they died. He knelt down to pick up some of the papers. Roxie was immediately by his side, licking his face, but Jordan pushed her away. And then the room tilted. Jordan fell backward, but his eyes were glued to the leather binding in front of him. He would recognize it anywhere, but he hadn't known that his father's journal was in the box of personal effects. For as long as he could remember, his dad had used an old leather book cover for his favorite collection of thoughts and inspirational stories. He'd quoted many of them to Jordan and Lexi when they were teenagers. The leather book cover became a sort of running joke because everything Dad quoted from the book might as well have come from the Bible. They weren't allowed to argue with the sentiment—listen and ponder were the strict rules Dad enforced. And all teasing aside, Jordan and Lexi had treasured many of those talks with their father.

The leather cover was chewed in pieces, separated from the book. Jordan looked around the room and saw ripped and slobbery pages strewn across the floor. Something in his heart came unhinged in that moment. Jordan clenched his jaw, but the scream inside his head reverberated against his skull.

"I can't do this anymore!" he cried.

Roxie came toward him and licked his hand. "No!" Jordan stepped away from her, shaking his head. "No! No more!"

The puppy looked at him and then lay on the floor, putting her head between her front paws, her brown eyes filled with confusion. Jordan turned away and grabbed his cell phone. Twenty minutes later, his assistant Cindy was loading Roxie up in the kennel. Jordan couldn't look at Roxie. It was all he could do to give Cindy the address to the animal shelter. He sent her with three-hundred dollars in cash and a request to get Roxie to Madison.

"But, sir, I don't think you should do this. Why don't you let me help you clean up the mess and it'll give you time to think it over?" Cindy asked.

"I can't do this anymore." Jordan walked away before she could argue further. He stomped into the house and slammed the door, but stopped to watch through the window as Cindy got into her car.

The minute Cindy drove away, Jordan wanted to race after the car and undo everything that had happened. He kept seeing Roxie's tail, wagging as she was loaded into the kennel. Madison would know what to do. She hated Jordan anyway; why not give her another reason to be sure of her hate?

Chapter 23

*M*adison's face was splotchy and her eyes were sore from crying by the time she'd explained everything to Sue.

"Darlin', are you sure you know what was going on tonight?" Sue asked. She patted Madison's back and her dark eyes searched Madison's face.

"I was there, wasn't I? He practically ignored me. He didn't even know that I'd left!" Madison cried.

Sue clicked her tongue and shook her head. "He made some big mistakes, that's fo' sure, but where was his heart tonight?"

Madison bit her lip, trying to think of how to answer the question. She wanted to be angry at Jordan, but a small part of her softened as she recalled the look of frustration and anguish on his face as he was pulled from their private dinner date into that room with Carlotta the vampire. If she were being truthful,

Jordan didn't look like he'd enjoyed a minute of those conversations. She frowned because she couldn't understand why Jordan couldn't have stood up to those people and reassured them that she was his girlfriend, not just his dog trainer.

A bell chimed out front, and Sue and Madison looked up. The shelter was technically closed. "I'll get it," Sue said, and ambled for the door.

Madison heard a bit of commotion and a dog yip, then make a mournful whining sound that tugged on Maddie's heartstrings. She stood and walked to the front, peeking around the corner. Madison recognized Jordan's assistant, Cindy, from her frequent visits to the house. She stood holding Roxie's leash as the pup whined.

"Yes, I'm sure," Cindy said as she handed the leash to Sue. "He said he just can't do it anymore."

In a moment, Madison realized what was happening. She stepped forward. "What happened? I don't believe he would really do this."

Cindy shook her head. "I've never seen him like this before. He was so upset, but not angry, just defeated. I tried to talk him out of it but I didn't want to lose my job. I hope you understand."

Madison took Roxie by the leash. "Thanks for bringing her by. We had a date that went really badly tonight." She looked down at Roxie and patted her head. "You can tell him I got the message."

Cindy shook her head. "That's not what this is about. I saw his office. Roxie practically destroyed it. There were papers

155

everywhere. I don't know if she did something else, but it looked like Jordan was ready to cry."

Madison felt guilt tightening her shoulders, but she rolled it off. Jordan had no right to act this way. "Let me give you my number. If you find out anything else, will you please let me know?"

Cindy hesitated, and then nodded. "Sure, I can do that."

They exchanged phone numbers and Madison took Roxie to the back. She rubbed behind the puppy's ears and felt more tears rising in the back of her throat. Sue came in a few minutes later and Madison looked at her and swiped a tear from her eye. "Why would he do this? I mean, I know it's my fault, but he didn't have to give up Roxie."

Sue patted Madison's back and then rubbed the top of Roxie's head. "You say you know this Jordan fellow?"

Madison shrugged. "Yes, I mean I thought I did."

Sue nodded. "Well, it sounded like he cared for you—maybe even loved you."

"And I left him there," Madison murmured. "He was so excited for tonight, and then everything fell apart. It reminded me of the times when my dad would make promises to me. He never kept his word."

Sue clicked her tongue. "It's bad business letting our pasts color our futures."

Madison's shoulders slumped. "I shouldn't have pushed him away."

"Honey, you had to take care of yourself, but did you give him a chance to explain or apologize?"

"He tried, but Sue, I can't go down that road again. I can't depend on a man who puts his job first."

Sue patted Madison's back. "Something else happened tonight. Something that made him think he couldn't take care of Roxie anymore. He's done something hasty, but don't you do the same. Give it some time."

Madison held Roxie close and tried to see the situation from Sue's perspective instead of through the lens of her own hurt. Had she been too hasty in turning Jordan away? Every time she tried to make sense of the evening, she felt more confused. What had happened to Jordan and the fragile changes he'd begun to make in his busy life?

Roxie licked Madison's cheek where a tear was trailing toward her lip. "I should've tried harder to understand him, huh?" she whispered to the puppy.

Roxie's tail thumped on the ground as Madison held her close and cried.

 **Chapter 24**

*J*ordan threw his hands up in the air, pushing all thoughts away. He had to clean up the mess. Face the past once and for all. He slipped on a pair of flip flops to avoid the glass on the floor. The office echoed with every slap of his flip flops against the floor. He stood in the doorway and surveyed the damage again, trying to find remnants of his father's book. He walked carefully through the debris and around his desk. Underneath the chair he found what he was looking for. A chunk of the book was still held together by the glue on the binding, even though the cover had been mostly torn off.

Jordan picked up the remains of the book. The leather cover was probably one of the first things Roxie had chewed. The flaps of the book cover were still intact, but the book was destroyed. Jordan turned the flap over and his finger caught the edge of a postcard tucked inside. His father's handwriting ran along the edge of the card. Jordan flipped it over. The postcard showed a familiar view of Lake Michigan, but when Jordan flipped it back over, his fingers trembled when he saw his own name on the top of the card. His chest constricted, begging him to take in a breath, but the world had stopped.

Lexi had been there when the police officer brought the box of personal items from the wreckage. She'd looked through the box and given it to him. At least Jordan thought she had examined the contents because Lexi had taken their mother's purse and retrieved the compact mirror with a hand-painted beach scene on the outside. But Lexi hadn't gone through the entire box. She never would have left their father's book in the bottom of the box if she had known it was there. Jordan had shoved the box in the bottom of his bedroom closet in his apartment, not able to go through the contents while the pain was so fresh. When he moved into his Lake Forest mansion a couple years later, the box had ended up in his office closet. Now Jordan held the postcard with his father's writing and he was terrified to read the words. He closed his eyes and blew out his breath, summoning courage that had been absent in every action that night. He opened his eyes and began reading.

> *Jordan,*
>
> *I'm proud of you son. Whatever you choose to do, I'll be happy for you. I just want you to be happy. There is so much more to life than work. I'm worried that you might lose your way if you don't find the right woman to guide you and remind you of how wonderful you already are. I'm sorry we haven't always agreed on things and I'm sorry that I*

pushed you too hard. You'll find your way and it will be the right one because your soul is meant for greatness.

> *Love,*
> *Dad*
>
> *P.S. Ralph says hi!*

There was no date on the letter. His father could have written it at any time, but the words sounded so different from the last conversation they'd had. Maybe Jordan hadn't listened as closely as he should have when his father spoke. He thought back on that conversation and most of what he could remember now was his father urging him to choose a route that would allow him to provide for a family and be happy.

And the postscript was yet another sign of how well his father knew him. Jordan had been so worried about Ralph and his declining health. He didn't want to put the dog down, but he hadn't wanted him to suffer either. At the time, Jordan was in a cheap apartment that didn't allow pets and his parents assured him that Ralph would be happier in the familiar surroundings where he'd lived his entire life.

It was still a terrible irony to Jordan that through the car accident, Ralph had been given a release from the decay of his earthly body while his parents had been robbed of so many years left to live.

Jordan's eyes burned and tears slipped from his lashes. He moved the paper closer, rereading the words that his father had penned. The right woman to guide you. That was Madison. Jordan knew that truth as sure as he knew that Roxie had saved his life that night in more ways than one. And he'd pushed them both away. The tears flowed and Jordan let them come.

He was completely alone, and as he sobbed like he hadn't done since his parents died, he realized that he didn't want to be alone anymore. He didn't want to get lost in the years of work building up a business and never have a family to come home to. Work wasn't the meaning of life. Jordan stood and washed his face with cool water. It was time to make some changes in his life and he wouldn't let another moment pass him by. Jordan didn't want to wait for a driver. He hurried from the house into the garage where his silver Aston Martin was parked. He sped to the edges of the city, hoping that he wasn't too late.

Madison pulled up some paperwork, looked at Roxie, and bit her trembling lip.

"Don't you dare check that puppy into this shelter," Sue said. "You take her home. This isn't over. He's hurting, and sometimes when people are hurting they lash out at those they love most."

"This proves that I was right," Madison fired back. "He doesn't really care about me, or Roxie, or anyone. All he cares about is his job!"

"You hurt him, honey, and people don't know how to deal with that kind of hurt." Sue shook her head. "You go on home, but you'd better think about something—Jordan has done a lot of good in this world because he works so hard. He doesn't know any other way, but it looked to me like you two were pretty happy there for a while. Are you sure you know his heart?"

Madison cried all the way home, with Roxie whining in the back seat, probably worrying that she was responsible for Madison's storm of emotions. When she got back to her apartment, she held Roxie until they both fell asleep in the recliner in her front room. Madison awoke to Roxie licking her face and the tears had flowed again. She had to protect herself, and so she had pushed Jordan away. There were so many signs that he didn't really want to change. Madison wasn't willing to play with fire when the scars from her burns were still visible in her mind's eye.

It sounded like Sue didn't believe Jordan was like Madison's father, but she hadn't been there at The Signature Room to see just how wrong the evening had gone. Madison realized something with a shuddering breath. In a way tonight was worse than all the times her father had stood her up, cancelled plans, and dodged responsibilities. It was worse because Jordan had been right there, a few feet away and ignored her. She felt small, like the insecure child she had been, and there was nothing that could make that feeling disappear.

Chapter 25

*J*ordan sent one text to Madison the day after his world crumbled around him: **I have changed and I know WHY. Give me one week and I'll answer your question.**

Madison didn't respond, but Jordan pretended that she still believed in him enough to give him one more chance.

Burke Enterprises was like a beehive that week with new hires coming in every day, more office spaces being reorganized and one meeting after the next. Jordan slept at the office twice and worked until the lines of reports swam before his eyes, but he pushed harder for Madison. By Friday, his entire life would change.

He consulted with several experts who cautioned him against the move because Burke Enterprises couldn't be successful without the driving force of Jordan Burke. But when he talked with Paul Redly, his mentor and friend had smiled and clapped Jordan on the back. "It's the hard choice son, but it's also the right one."

"Then why is everyone telling me it's the wrong move?"

"Because they don't know your path," Paul said. "They can only give advice on a path they understand."

Jordan kept those words with him throughout the week and recalled them each time he thought about Madison and the questions she'd asked him. He knew the answer to his why now and he would prove it to her next time he saw her.

He left his office for an extended lunch break on Thursday so that he could call his sister. He decided to take Madison's advice and confide his deepest regret to Lexi. Once Lexi was on the phone, Jordan told her everything about that night and the argument he'd had with their father.

"Oh, Jordy. I'm sorry that you've been blaming yourself. It wasn't your fault." Her voice sounded like she might be crying.

"I believe that now, but I still regret how I treated Dad."

"Dad pushed us hard and he knew that sometimes he crossed the line. I'm sure he forgave you. He and mom were probably talking about how much they love their headstrong children when the accident happened."

Jordan chuckled. "You didn't ever fight with dad, did you?"

Now it was Lexi's turn to laugh. "Of course I did. Sometimes Dad was right, and sometimes I was right, but let me tell you something."

"I'm listening."

"Dad was so proud of you. He told me all the time that he knew you'd find your way."

"Then why did he fight with me about what I was doing?"

"Because he was worried about you, and he loved you," Lexi hesitated. "Mom and I talked a lot too, and she told me. I thought you knew. I wish you would have talked to me about this sooner."

Jordan sighed. "I'm glad we could talk now."

"Are you going to be okay Jordy? Is everything okay with you and Madison?"

Jordan's throat tightened. "I hope that it will be. I'm making some pretty big changes so that I will have time for a family because I love her."

"You love her?!" Lexi's voice pitched higher with excitement. "I'm so happy for you. Have you told her yet?"

"No, but I'm going to very soon. I have some pretty big news for you about Burke Enterprises."

Lexi listened as Jordan explained to her how his life would be completely different from now on. When he said goodbye to his sister, Jordan felt confident that he had made the right decisions in his company. Lexi told him that she would pray for him and Madison to be together, and Jordan echoed that prayer as he drove back to his office.

On Friday, Jordan closed his computer, stood and stretched and felt a world of worry drain off his shoulders and pool on the floor. What was done was done. He smiled and stepped away from his office. He felt like he was leaving a piece of himself there on his desk, and he was okay with that. It was time to reinvent Jordan Burke.

He drove himself outside of the city to a run-down warehouse near a nice upper-class neighborhood. There were dozens of workers there hauling away garbage, cleaning, painting, and repairing windows. The back of the lot had patches of grass in a vacant dirt yard and several maple trees lined the property. "It's perfect," he said quietly as he walked around the building.

Cindy held the leash of a beautiful golden retriever that was almost a year old. She paced back and forth across the lot with the dog. Lexi's old assistant, Shawn Halstrom, had his hand atop the head of a German shepherd. When he'd heard about Jordan's plans, he'd been one of the first to volunteer to help. Jordan walked up and took the leash from Cindy.

"Thanks for helping me make this happen."

Cindy smiled. "She'll be here any minute." She walked toward the front of the building, weaving around the workers. Jordan's heart pounded in his chest. He'd never wanted anything so badly in his life, and he prayed that he'd done the right thing.

Madison pulled up to the old warehouse, curious at the bustle of activity surrounding it. When one of her top clients had asked to meet here for a training session, Madison had been hesitant until they assured her that the place was under new ownership and would be perfect to begin training a new service dog.

As she got out of the car, she saw Cindy approaching her and Madison looked around, searching for Jordan. Cindy's face lit up with a big smile. "I'm so glad you're here. Your new client is around back."

"Wait a minute," Madison said. "Did you set this up?"

Cindy nodded. "I hope you don't mind. I knew you were the best one for this job. Come on."

Madison's curiosity edged up several notches. She followed Cindy around the back of the building and sucked in a breath when she saw Jordan crouching near a golden retriever. He wore a gray t-shirt and jeans, and he stood to face her. Something was different about him. Maybe a new haircut?

"Hi, Maddie." Jordan waved and licked his lips.

"What are you doing here? Is this some kind of trick?" Madison put her hand on her hip.

"No, I heard that there was an incredibly talented woman starting a business for training service dogs."

Madison tilted her head, looking from one dog to the other. Cindy and Shawn looked like they were trying hard not to all-out beam at her. "Okay?"

"And I've been working too hard lately—well, forever really," Jordan said. "I decided it was time to make some permanent changes in my life."

"So, you got another dog?"

Jordan chuckled. "Yes, but first I made a career change."

It took a moment for Madison to process his words. "What?"

"I made a career change. I had planned to tell you how I sold off a huge company to free up more time that night at the restaurant, but everything went wrong. I want you to know how sorry I am for the pain I caused you. Because of what happened, I realized that I couldn't just sell off one company. I needed to do something bigger—more meaningful—for you." He lifted the leash in his hand. "I am no longer acting CEO of Burke Enterprises. We hired a new CEO who will be running everything. I've always loved dogs and I want to learn how to train service dogs. My friends helped me find this warehouse and within a few weeks it'll be ready for you—to start your new business."

Madison looked from Jordan to Shawn and Cindy and then at the dogs wagging their tails happily. She opened her mouth and shook her head. "Jordan, you don't have to do this. I understand how important your company is."

Jordan handed the leash to Cindy and took three steps toward Madison. "It's already done. My company was important, but you are more important—the most important part of my life."

"But your company?"

Jordan reached out and took her hand. "My company is still my company, but from now on it will run without me. In fact, I couldn't go back now if I wanted to because we put a whole new board in place along with the CEO."

Madison shook her head slowly, trying to comprehend what he had said. "You're not going back?"

Jordan grinned. "I'm not ever going back. No more trips to China, no late night phone calls. I'll be financially independent, but I'm making time for the people that I love."

Madison's heart fluttered when he said the "L" word and looked at her, his green eyes dancing. He took a step closer to her.

"Madison, I figured out the answer to your question. I know why now."

"You do?" She held her breath, waiting for him to answer the question that she had asked him in so many different ways. Jordan had never been able to answer her when she asked why he worked so hard, why he had given up his life for his company, and why he couldn't slow down. He had started to show her why, but she leaned forward, eager to hear him tell her why.

"I worked because it was the only thing that made sense in my life, especially after my parents died. But that wasn't my why, I didn't realize until I started dating you that I didn't have a why. Money and success are great, but they aren't my why. *You* are my why. I've changed my life because I want you to be sure—absolutely certain—that you are my why."

She glanced down at his fingers covering hers. "Is this real?"

"Yep, there's just one thing left that I think will convince you how real this is." Jordan nodded to someone behind Madison.

Madison heard a yip and turned to see Roxie running toward them. Sue was a few paces behind, holding the leash she'd just unclipped. The black lab streaked toward Jordan, her mouth hanging open and pink tongue reaching for his face. Jordan laughed and hugged Roxie. He looked up at Madison and the joy in his eyes touched her heart.

"So you're ready to take your dog back?" Madison asked lightly, covering the emotion she felt welling up inside her.

"Only if you're part of the package." Jordan stood and reached for her hand again. "I love you, Maddie. I need you. You helped me know what living really is and I don't want to go down this path without you."

Jordan loved her, and he'd changed his whole life for her. A tiny part of her brain felt scared, but Madison gazed into his eyes, taking in everything he'd said. His words were sincere and Madison felt the weight of them, the rightness of them settle on her heart. She squeezed his hand. "I love you, too."

Roxie yipped and ran a quick circle around Jordan and Madison as they embraced. Jordan held Madison close and whispered in her ear, "I promise my heart won't ever stray again. It's yours."

"I believe you, Jordy." Madison giggled when he raised his eyes and leaned in to kiss her.

Roxie yipped again, and Jordan reached a hand down to pat the puppy's head. He grinned, and then pulled Madison closer, covering her mouth with a gentle kiss that held a promise of a future that she definitely wanted to enjoy with this man.

The End

Keep reading for a sneak peek of Lexi's story…#1 Burke Billionaire Romance

Hawaiian Masquerade

Chapter 1

Lexi stared at the tube of cadmium red oil paint hanging from the shelf, remembering how expensive that color had seemed in college. She grabbed it and ten additional tubes in a rainbow of colors—the first step on a new path in life. The squeaking wheel of the shopping cart gave voice to the trepidation crawling up her spine, telling her she was nuts for leaving behind a life that most people claimed they wanted. But Lexi knew something that most people didn't: millions and millions of dollars did not create a wellspring of happiness. Cold hard cash was, in fact, cold and hard.

Kauai was not cold. The brilliant sunshine and perfumed air was freely available to everyone on the island. Roadways were drenched in color from vibrant greens to bright pinks and accented with the red dirt Kauai was known for. Lexi studied the brushes available and chose a long-handled round brush that would help her recreate the beautiful landscapes of the island. Now if she could find a few canvases, she would be ready to paint on the beach outside her home. She turned down another aisle and saw a display of white rectangles and squares. They were wrapped in plastic, but Lexi ran her finger along the edges; the rough feel of a blank canvas and the possibility it represented brought back pleasant memories.

A toddler's shrill cry snapped her out of her musings. She steered her cart around a stack of twelve-by-eighteen-inch canvases and found the source. The little girl couldn't have been more than two years old, tiny with fine black hair pulled back in pigtails. Her red hibiscus-print dress set off dark caramel skin, and even as her wail intensified, Lexi found herself admiring the pretty Polynesian girl.

That's when she noticed that the toddler was alone. Lexi glanced around, but this area of the store was empty. She stepped forward carefully and crouched in front of the girl. "Sweetie, are you lost?"

As soon as the words left her mouth, the little girl held out her arms and reached for Lexi. She sniffled, melting Lexi's heart as she carefully picked up the child. She looked down the aisle, hoping to see the little girl's mother, but at the same time nervous that the mother would think her daughter was being kidnapped. Lexi patted the girl's back, and she snuggled closer. Swallowing against the sudden lump in her throat, Lexi focused on the task at hand.

Turning slowly to scan the store again, she saw a man with dark hair, a chiseled jawline, and a worried crease in his forehead. He was tall with golden-brown skin and wore a green tank top that showed off his finely sculpted biceps. Something shifted in Lexi's heart. It thumped hard twice, and blood rose to her cheeks. The man stared back at her, his face open, revealing an arc of emotions as he took in the sight of the little girl and Lexi—wonder, admiration, curiosity, and something else she couldn't define.

She stepped forward, eyebrows raised in question. "Is she yours?"

His dark hair was spiked on top and close-shaven on the sides. He sported a bit of scruff that Lexi could only describe as sexy. One side of his mouth lifted, and he shook his head. "No, is she lost?"

"Yes, she was crying right over here, and I've stayed put for a minute hoping her mom would show up looking for her."

He turned around in a slow circle, repeating the search Lexi had undertaken moments before, having a better view over the shelves because he was taller. Oh, so tall and sculpted. "I can help you find her parents. This store isn't that big. Maybe they haven't missed her yet."

Lexi's brow furrowed in protest as she struggled to rein in her emotions. It had been at least three minutes since she'd heard the toddler's cries, and five minutes was like an eternity in a child's world—surely it would feel just as long for a frantic parent searching for her child. She gently patted the girl's back. "It's okay, sweetie, I know what it feels like to be lost," she murmured. Then she realized that the man was standing close enough to hear her. She straightened, cleared her throat, and spoke louder. "We'll help you."

The man pointed to the other side of the store. "I'll go this way, you go that way?"

"That's a good idea." Lexi smiled, and her stomach flipped when the man returned her smile. The little girl moved her head, quiet and warm in Lexi's arms.

The man walked quickly across the store, and Lexi went in the other direction. There was only one other shopper, an old man with a handful of charcoal and sketch pads. Lexi smiled at him, and he winked at her and the little girl. "Beautiful kaikamahine."

Lexi nodded, appreciating the melodic Hawaiian language. The man saw them as mother and daughter, which was a stretch considering Lexi's fair skin, blond hair, and green eyes. She held the child close. They were two lost souls trying to find something to keep them safe. Lexi was certain she'd find the little girl's mother, but what could Lexi find that would fill the need in her heart?

"Here she is," someone said from behind Lexi. She turned around and saw that the dark-haired man was leading a Polynesian woman with long dark hair toward her. "Safe and sound."

"Keilani! Oh, baby," the woman said. "I'm so glad you're okay."

The little girl immediately sat up and reached her arms out. She cried for a few seconds, clinging to her mother, clutching her light cotton shirt.

"Mahalo. Oh, thank you so much for finding my baby," the woman gushed.

"She's a sweetheart," Lexi said. "She wanted me to hold her, and that seemed to help while we looked for you."

"One minute she was there, and then she was gone. You know how kids are." The woman patted her daughter's back. "Keilani, say thank you to the beautiful lady who found you," the woman said, looking down at her daughter with a smile.

The toddler looked at Lexi and held her hand out, moving it back and forth. Then she giggled and blew Lexi a kiss.

Lexi pretended to catch the kiss in the air and patted her cheek. "Thank you, Keilani. Have fun shopping."

She waved at the little girl, then let her hand drop to her side. That's when she noticed the man who had helped her standing quietly next to the end cap of paintbrushes on aisle seven. "You really get the credit for finding her," Lexi said. "Thanks for hunting down the lost mother."

He grinned. "Glad to help out a tourist when I can."

"But I'm not a tourist," Lexi replied. "I just moved here."

One eyebrow lifted, and Lexi noticed a shift in his brown eyes, as if he were seeing her for the first time. He held out his hand. "That's great news. Aloha, and welcome to Kauai. I'm Derek Mitchell."

They shook hands, and a sensation like warm, salty spray went up her arm. When they broke contact, she immediately craved his touch again. What was happening to her? The first hot guy to shake her hand had her thinking of moonlight walks on the beach and kisses in the sand. She decided that she was smitten with the *idea* of this Hawaiian guy. She needed a can of chocolate-covered macadamia nuts and a long bath, not a man. Still, she smiled broadly and returned the introduction. "I'm Lexi Burke, no longer from Chicago."

Derek wrinkled his nose. "Man, that place is cold. Good choice coming here in March. The weather will only get better from now until October."

"I'm counting on it," Lexi replied.

"Are you an artist?" Derek asked, motioning to the growing stack of supplies in Lexi's cart, which she'd left in the middle of the aisle.

"I wish." Lexi laughed as she grabbed the handle. "Maybe in a different lifetime—or maybe now. I love art, and I need to refocus some of my energy. Drawing and painting used to be a passion of mine, before the nine-to-five killed it."

Derek nodded. "I get that. The good thing about this place is it unwinds all that tension, and creativity leaks out from everywhere." He tipped his head to the side. "Since you're new, I'll let you in on a secret. Drive over to Hanapepe tomorrow—Friday night is the local art night—and you'll see what I mean."

"Hmm, I may just do that." Lexi gave Derek her canned response to every invite from the male species. And then she realized that he was being friendly. Maybe she could go . . . but then she might run into him, and he was too good-looking with that bronzed skin and his relaxed stance that seemed to say, *I don't have any idea what my looks do to your pulse rate.* Yep. Derek was on her list of things not to encounter in Kauai. Her fingertips drummed along the plastic-wrapped handle of her shopping cart, trying to keep up with her racing heart. It was time to make a quick exit. "Thanks again for your help. Maybe I'll see you around the island sometime."

"Good luck with the painting." Derek lifted one hand and let it fall. He had a stack of frames tucked under his other arm.

After checking out and packing the supplies into her Jeep, Lexie wished she hadn't been so skittish around Derek and missed the opportunity to reciprocate his interest in her new hobby. He'd spoken about creativity, and judging by the frames and his knowledge of the Hanapepe street fair, he was probably an artist himself. There she was, thinking about him again. Derek was just another piece of man candy Lexi didn't want to taste, even if he'd been kind and genuine at the store. She shouldn't be mean to him just because she carried a chip on her shoulder the size of the Sears Tower. She could give him the benefit of the doubt. Derek was quite possibly delicious on the inside, too.

Then again, so was the authentic Hawaiian shaved ice Lexi was going to pick up at Hee Fat General Store. Yes, ice covered in sugar sitting on top of a mountain of thick ice cream would definitely do the trick to keep Lexi's mind from wandering into dangerous territory.

Learn more about *Hawaiian Masquerade* at www.rachellechristensen.com

Note to the Reader

Thank you for reading my novel! I hope you enjoyed Jordan and Madison AND Roxie's story as much as I enjoyed writing it. I have a special place in my heart for the darling little black lab puppy who inspired the character of Roxie in this book. She's my dog and we rescued her from the shelter at just four months old. Our Roxey has taught us so much in the past year. I've always been a dog lover, but I forgot how destructive one little puppy can be! Roxey reminded me why animals are an important part of our human existence. They teach all of us, adults and children, about unconditional love. Now, I have five children so I know a thing or two about unconditional love, but what Roxey taught me was a reminder of the innocence of children, who like puppies will give love unconditionally no matter what. It is our responsible to return that love.

If this story has inspired you, I would encourage you to contact your local animal shelter to find out what you can do to help these animals who are in need of love. And if you enjoyed this story, I would greatly appreciate it if you would leave a review on Amazon or Goodreads. Each and every review is important to the success of my books. Thank you in advance for your support!

Acknowledgements

I have always wanted to be a writer, clear back to the days of my childhood when I would sit in my pasture and compose poetry. When I first started attending writing conferences, I made a goal that I wanted to have twenty published books in the next fifteen years. I am so thrilled to report that you have just finished reading my twenty-first published book!

There are so many people to thank that I would need to write another book to fill the pages of people who have touched my writing career in some way. There are countless author friends, writing instructors, mentors, editors, and READERS who have impacted my career. THANK YOU! I wouldn't be where I am today without the help of hundreds of people who believed in me and my writing talent.

For this book, I owe a huge thanks to my editor, Daniel Coleman, who helped me get this manuscript in shape. I'm grateful to my writing group who helped me brainstorm this plot and provided such great feedback on all the sticky points from the outline to the cover. Thank you to Cami Checketts, Kimberly Krey, Lucy McConnell, Cindy Anderson, Daniel Banner, Taylor Hart, Jennifer Youngblood, Sarah Gay, Kimberley Montpetit, Liz Isaacson, and Christine Kersey. Thank you to Steven Novak for another fabulous cover!

I have so much gratitude to my family—my husband and five children—you constantly lift me up and encourage me. I love you! Thank you to my mom and dad—two book lovers who have instilled a love of the written word in me that will never fade. I love you so much!

I'm thankful to God for the blessings He continues to give to me each day, and for the gentle reminders of what is most important in life.

Photo by Erin Summerill

About the Author

*R*achelle is a mother of five who writes mystery/suspense, nonfiction, and women's fiction. She solves the case of the missing shoe on a daily basis. She enjoys raising chickens and laughing with her husband. She graduated cum laude from Utah State University with a degree in psychology and a minor in music.

Rachelle is the award-winning author of twenty books, including *The Soldier's Bride (a Kindle Scout Selection)*, *Diamond Rings Are Deadly Things*, *Hawaiian Masquerade*, and *Christmas Kisses: An Echo Ridge Anthology*. Her novella, "Silver Cascade Secrets," was included in the Rone Award–winning *Timeless Romance Anthology, Fall Collection*.

Join Rachelle's VIP mailing list to learn more about upcoming books and get your free book at www.rachellechristensen.com.